BLIND DROP

Colonel Vivian Rowlands, renowned for his wartime exploits in Yugoslavia, was a hero, but his son Charles wasn't. All Charles wanted was to be left in peace in his Suffolk retreat and write. When a dawn call from Scotland Yard tells him that his father has been killed by a car bomb, Charles's peaceful life is shattered. However hard he tries not to get involved, he is drawn ever more deeply into a world of intrigue and violence where nothing, even heroism, is quite what it seems.

JAMES NICHOLAS

BLIND DROP

Complete and Unabridged

LINFORD
Leicester

First published in Great Britain in 1981 by
Robert Hale Limited
London

First Linford Edition
published 2003
by arrangement with
Robert Hale Limited
London

British Library CIP Data

Nicholas, James
    Blind drop.—Large print ed.—
Linford mystery library
1. Detective and mystery stories
2. Large type books
I. Title
823.9'14 [F]

ISBN 0–7089–9470–9

Published by
F. A. Thorpe (Publishing)
Anstey, Leicestershire

Set by Words & Graphics Ltd.
Anstey, Leicestershire
Printed and bound in Great Britain by
T. J. International Ltd., Padstow, Cornwall

This book is printed on acid-free paper

09022770

1

It was Wednesday morning in late November when the insistent yelping of the telephone, distant yet compelling, dragged me from the womb-like comfort of the electric blanket to face the sub-zero darkness of the world beyond my bed.

Carefully I disentangled myself from Frances, who grunted and turned over without waking. Then I eased my legs from beneath the dead weight of two cats, which didn't wake, either.

There was an old travelling clock on the chair that served as a bedside table. It had a luminous dial, and I calculated, allowing for the intuitive advances Frances made to compensate for the indeterminate amount it lost, the time was probably five o'clock.

'Bastards!' I said aloud. Frances grunted again, but the cats ignored me.

There was a man in the village, a farm worker, who always got up at five. I admired him for it, but I objected to getting his alarm calls, which I did about once a month when the operators at Ipswich muddled my number with his. I objected very strongly, especially on a winter's morning like this, when I had not reached my bed until two, in circumstances that demanded a long period of undisturbed rest and recuperation. This time I was determined to give those dozey operators such a blast that it would cripple them for life.

The air was freezing, and I was naked. I fumbled about and located my old dressing gown on its nail driven into the oaken crossbeam which supported the roof. I couldn't find my slippers, so, barefoot, I went backwards down the steep, perilous wooden stairs into the living room.

I switched on the light. In the cavernous fireplace a large section of diseased elm was still glowing red in the basket grate. Three cushions from the sofa were on the floor across the hearth, and strewn around were outer clothes and underclothes, coffee cups, glasses and an empty whisky bottle. The still, stale air reeked of cigarettes and debauchery.

The television, mute and blind, now, reminded me that Tuesday evening had started off with myself and Frances innocently ensconced in separate chairs, watching one of the old films for which we shared an addiction. This one had been 'The Thin Man', and we had ended up on the cushions in front of the fire with me playing a very creditable Nick, and Frances overacting outrageously as Nora.

I crossed the disordered room to reach the tiny hall and the telephone. In that confined space, its clamour was like a physical blow. I snatched up the receiver.

'No!' I shouted. 'This is not 412!'

There was no response. All I could hear were the usual buzzings and clickings which were an intrinsic part of the telephone system in that remote part of Suffolk.

'This is 421,' I yelled. 'Four . . . two . . . one . . . '

From what seemed a long way away, a man's voice said, 'Is that Mr Rowlands?'

'Yes,' I said. 'Yes. What about it? Don't you know what time it is?'

'This is the Metropolitan Police,' said the voice.

'The what?'

'Scotland Yard. Hold the line, please.'

In my bemused, sleep-sodden state, geared to do battle with idiot telephone operators, I reacted slowly. Scotland Yard? Me? At five in the morning? It must be a mistake, or someone playing a despicable practical joke. I hesitated, tempted to slam down the receiver and crawl back to bed; but the beginnings of panic clutched me and held me there, listening to the ghostly noises until I heard another voice, deeper and more authoritative than the first asking, 'Mr Rowlands? Mr Charles Rowlands?'

'Yes, yes,' I snapped. 'Who the hell are you? It's five o'clock in the morning, for Christ's sake!'

'Barker,' said the man. 'Chief Superintendent. I'm sorry to call you at this hour, Mr Rowlands.'

'I should think you are!' I said, but the aggression was seeping out of me. The panic was taking hold.

'Your father,' said Barker, 'would be Colonel Vivian Rowlands. Am I correct?'

I swallowed back the nervous lump that had risen to constrict my throat.

'Yes,' I said. 'What is it? What's happened?'

'I'm afraid I have some bad news, Mr Rowlands.'

'I . . . I can't hear you very well,' I said. 'It's a terrible line.' But I had heard him; I had heard him all too clearly.

'You must prepare yourself for a shock, sir,' said Barker. 'Your father has been involved in an accident — a sort of accident.'

'Oh my God!' I said. 'What's he done this time?'

'I don't quite know how to tell you this,' said Barker. 'A car was blown up in the Bloomsbury district about an hour ago. We have reason to believe your father was in it.'

'In it?' I cried. 'In it? You mean he's been killed?'

'If it was him, sir, yes, I'm sorry to say I do.'

My brain refused to function; I simply couldn't grasp what he was talking about. A car blown up? A car!

'Not the old Rover?' I said.

'I'm sorry?'

'The car!' I said. 'The car — was it an old Rover?'

'It was a Rover, certainly,' said Barker.

All I could think of in those first stunned moments was the stately old car my father had cherished so long. Like a faithful dog it had acquired its master's personality.

'He'd had that car for thirty years!' I said. 'Thirty bloody years!'

There was something warm and soft bunting against my bare ankles. It was Clive, the black cat with the white paws, who had left the bed to investigate what all the commotion was about. He jumped on to the table and tried to climb up my chest to reach the telephone. I believe he thought it was some small animal I was cuddling to my face, and he was jealous. I tried to push him off, but he draped himself round my neck like a fur collar.

'Are you there, Mr Rowlands?' asked Barker.

'Yes . . . ' I said, struggling with one hand to pull Clive away. He was purring ecstatically. 'I'm a bit . . . I can't think straight at the moment.'

'Understandable,' said Barker. 'Take your time.'

'Tell me what happened,' I said.

'All we know,' said Barker, 'is that the car was parked in Chester Passage, off Bedford Square. At approximately ten minutes to four this morning, it blew up . . . presumably due to a bomb. A man was in the car . . . a man we have reason to think was Colonel Rowlands.'

'Reason to think?' I said. 'Then you don't know?'

'There has been no positive identification at this stage,' said Barker. 'The explosion was — well, it was fairly massive, and then there must have been a lot of petrol about. There was a fire . . . '

'Oh, my God!' I said. 'What do you want me to do?'

'It would help if you could come to London, sir. As soon as possible.'

'Of course,' I said. 'Of course. I'll come at once. I could be there . . . I don't know . . . I should be able to make it by half-past ten.'

'Come to Scotland Yard,' he said. 'Ask for me, Chief Superintendent Barker. By the way, if you have any calls from the media, refer them to me. We haven't released anything officially yet . . . but you never know.'

I put the phone down, and when I turned I found that Frances was standing in the doorway. She had a blanket draped around her and she was holding Sarah, the tortoiseshell cat, in her arms.

'What's all that, then?' she asked.

'My father,' I said. 'My poor bloody father. Some bastards have blown him to smithereens!' And then I began to cry, choking sobs which frightened Clive who leapt down from my shoulders and ran to Frances for protection.

'I'll make some tea,' said Frances.

2

From an early age it had been impressed upon me that my father was a hero, or, to be more precise, that he had been a hero. By the time I was old enough for the impression to register, my father's career as a hero was very definitely a thing of the past. It was a past, to me, bewilderingly remote and unreal, and was important simply because his historic heroism had not been succeeded by any other significant occupation.

He was not a communicative person. He was moody, monosyllabic and very English in his reticence. He seemed to be especially averse to talking about those war-time exploits which had established him as a hero. The most I could extract from him was that certain aspects had not been exactly a picnic, others had been a trifle hairy, or, occasionally, a bit sticky. It was my Italian mother who compensated for this taciturn understatement with

Latin extravagance.

If my mother were to be believed — and until I reached my cynical adolescence, I did believe her implicitly — my father had been a sort of Lawrence of Yugoslavia. With some slight assistance from someone called Tito — 'a factory worker, caro, quite a common sort of man' — he had led the brave Partisans in their desperate struggle to free themselves from the cruel yoke of German tyranny. My mother never mentioned the cruel yoke of Italian tyranny, or that Tito and his Partisans were Communists. She had a superb talent for disregarding awkward facts.

My mother's version of events, edited, glamorised and exaggerated as it undoubtedly was, contained more than a grain of truth.

The bare facts were that in April, 1943, young Captain Rowlands of the Special Operations Executive, was dropped by parachute into occupied Yugoslavia. He was dropped 'blind', which meant, in effect, that he was tossed out of a Whitley bomber in the middle of the night, with no exact idea of where he would land or what would happen to him when he did. Tossed out with him was a Sergeant Wireless Operator, whose function would be to transmit back to SOE headquarters in Cairo my father's reports on the confused activities of the Yugoslav Resistance fighters.

Intelligence leaking out of Yugoslavia at the time was sparse and unreliable, but it was known that there were two main resistance groups. One, loyal to the King and Government in exile in London, was led by Colonel Mihailovic, and the other was a revolutionary Communist force under Josip Broz, better known by his code name Tito.

It had been British policy to support Mihailovic, but after Soviet Russia came into the war on the Allied side, his activities became increasingly dubious, and there were suspicions that he was collaborating with the enemy to crush Tito. A previous British mission, two officers and two NCO's, who had been sent to Mihailovic, had disappeared without trace, and there were strong suspicions that they had either been murdered or betrayed to the enemy.

The area of Montenegro over which my father was dropped was thought to be in the hands of Tito's Liberation Army. This may have been true at the time the operation was planned, but in the interim, Hitler had ordered an all out offensive to crush the Communist resistance once and for all. Tito and the remnants of his ill-equipped and hopelessly outnumbered Partisans had been forced to retreat and take refuge in the caves and gorges of the wild, inaccessible mountains. The enemy strategy was to keep them bottled up, and to starve them into submission by denying them the support of the civilian population on whom they depended for supplies and recruits.

A campaign of terror was waged against the local people. Anyone suspected of helping or even of sympathising with the Partisans was shot out of hand. Whole villages were burnt to the ground; cattle were slaughtered and wells poisoned. Thousands of peasants fled before this relentless onslaught, and many sought refuge with the Partisans in their mountain caves, where food was already desperately short, and water had to be fetched, in goatskins, under the cover of night, from rivers constantly patrolled by enemy troops.

My father and the sergeant came down in the foothills and found that the Germans were waiting for them. The sergeant, hampered by the heavy wireless equipment, to which he clung with foolhardy courage, was shot and killed almost immediately. My father managed to reach the cover of some woods, but the following morning he was found by tracker dogs and taken prisoner. He was treated as a spy, interrogated and tortured by Gestapo agents, and finally told he was to be sent to Germany for execution.

On the journey, the train in which he was being taken to Berlin was attacked by Partisan saboteurs. In the confusion he escaped, killing two of his SS guards. He was wounded in the leg and for several days he crawled in agony through the forests until he came to a remote hamlet, where he was cared for, hidden in a barn and eventually taken by a secret route to the Partisan headquarters in the mountains.

All this I had pieced together, partly from my mother's romantic stories, and partly from reading more factual histories of the Yugoslav conflict. Once, when I suggested to my father that his own experiences would make a thrilling book, and that perhaps I could help him write it, his curiously gentle eyes grew hard and metallic.

'Why drag all that up?' he said curtly. 'Best forgotten.'

The trouble was, as I had realised long before, that, however much he might wish to, my father could not forget. For him, the mayhem and the murder were still going on. Disturbing evidence of his alienation manifested itself at night whilst he slept. He suffered from terrible, recurrent nightmares during which his customary reserve broke down completely, and he shouted, screamed, swore and thrashed about, wrestling with phantasmal enemies.

As a child, awoken by the uproar, to

which my mother added a shrill, hysterical counterpoint, I listened paralysed with fear, and at the same time, was beset with a sense of guilt, as though I were eaves-dropping on something peculiarly intimate and private. When the crisis passed, there would follow a period of weird silence. Then I would hear my mother whilst muttering tearful imprecations to the Virgin, creep towards the kitchen to make the tea laced with brandy which she always administered after these frenzies. She invariably paused to peep into my room; I always pretended to be fast asleep. I was ashamed for her to know that I had overheard.

My father did not work in the sense that other fathers seemed to work. Apart from a small disability pension, he had a private income derived from what had once been the Rowlands' family business, woollen mills in Bradford. My mother, too, had money of her own and the prospect of inheriting a great deal more. We weren't rich, but I suppose we were what is known as comfortably off. At any rate, there seemed no necessity for my father to earn a living.

Immediately after the war, when he came back to England with his Italian bride, he did, for a short time, have what might be called a proper job. It was some sort of temporary appointment at the Foreign Office, obtained on the strength of his war record and his knowledge of Serbo-Croat. This job came to an abrupt end when I was about six years old. One morning, as I was to learn many years later, he quietly left his desk and locked himself in the lavatory. Here he swallowed a large quantity of aspirins, washing them down with half a bottle of whisky.

It was the whisky which probably saved his life. It made him horribly sick, and the noise attracted attention. He was hurriedly bundled off to hospital, and the cover story put out that he had fainted. At that time, before all the scandals, attempting to commit suicide in the Foreign Office's sacred lavatories was looked upon as an unpardonable breach of gentlemanly behaviour.

For six months he was in a private clinic in Hampstead, and when he emerged, drugged, electrocuted and analysed, his superiors at the F.O. urged upon him the benefit he would derive from a quiet, rural existence, far removed from the pressures of London. We left our little house in Chelsea and moved to a rented Georgian rectory with ten acres near Diss in Norfolk. Here, my father pottered about breeding a few horses, at which he was quite successful, and embarking with sporadic enthusiasm on other projects apparently appropriate to ten acres, such as mushroom cultivation and broiler hens, at which he was not.

My mother hated the house, which was damp, decaying and infested with a breed of spiders remarkable for their size and impudence. She not only had a horror of spiders, she also loathed the bleak winds and the flat, Norfolk landscape. She had no interest in horses or country pursuits. She was a citizen of Rome, and she pined for people to chatter to, theatres, concerts and parties to dress up for. She needed the stimulus, the vital bustle of a great city, just as much as my father, or so he had been persuaded, needed the lonely emptiness of the country. Life at Diss was not the sort of existence my mother had envisaged when, as a decorative, amateur nurse, she had fallen in love with the handsome British war hero who had been one of her patients at the Roman palazzo which the victorious Allies had requisitioned as a convalescent home for officers.

My father's second breakdown occurred during my last term at school, at a time when a fierce dissension was raging about my future. It seemed that I was fated to be the cause of contention between my parents. There had been an earlier battle over the choice of school. My mother was determined I should go to the Catholic school, Uplands; my father favoured the Protestant Repton, where he himself had been educated. My mother prevailed, not so much on theological, as on the more mundane and practical grounds, that my rich Italian grandfather would be pleased. Now the argument centred on what I should do when I left Uplands.

My father wanted me to go up to his old college at Cambridge, but I had decided I wanted to be an artist; in fact, I was convinced that I was already an artist, and I had entered into a conspiracy with my mother to thwart my father, and to study art at the Slade.

Probably the breakdown had nothing to do with me or the quarrel about my career, but it left me, nevertheless, with an unpleasant mixture of resentment and guilt.

This time my father's breakdown took the form of cutting his wrist with a razor while in the bath. Whether he actually intended to kill himself, I don't know. If he had, I would have thought he would have locked the bathroom door, have chosen a time when he was alone in the house, and made rather less noise about it. These are conclusions I arrived at later, partly, no doubt to assuage my sense of guilt, and stiffen my determination to defy his wishes. It was while he was once again a patient in the psychiatric clinic that I became a student at the Slade School of Art.

From that time, guilt and my father became closely associated in my mind.

Irrationally, I felt that I was to blame for his mania. I was aware that I had always been a grave disappointment to him, and that if I had not been me, but an entirely different sort of son, it might at least have mitigated his trauma. I was useless at games, terrified of horses, scared out of my wits by guns and sympathetic towards foxes. When it came to fighting — sticking up for yourself, my father called it — I was an abject coward, and I still am.

I was delicate; I was limp and artistic; I was sensitive, wrote poetry, painted and went on marches with the object of Banning the Bomb. I was not the son in whom a man like Colonel Vivian Rowlands could take an interest, much less a pride.

To my mother, on the other hand, I was a walking miracle. She indulged me outrageously, protected me from what we both considered my father's philistinism, and encouraged me in the very pursuits he found most aggravating.

And now he was dead. They both were dead, but she, at least, had died in her beloved Rome, while he had ended as a charred horror in a Bloomsbury back-street. There was a dreadful inevitability about it, as though I had always known something like this would happen, and that in an obscure way I would be to blame.

3

The village was called Duck End and the house Duck End Farmhouse. It had a thatched roof and what estate agents call 'a wealth of old oak and period features'. It also had all those things estate agents don't talk about — like dry rot, rising damp, woodworm and a ghost Frances had invented for it. Prominent amongst the things it didn't have was main drainage.

The house was on the outskirts of the village, and although the farm part had shrunk to half an acre, it was still surrounded by farmland, and it didn't matter to me that this was now owned by a pension fund. The nearest neighbours were a quarter of a mile away, an elderly couple called Doyne. Mrs Doyne came in two mornings a week to clear up some of the mess, and her husband — Dad, she called him — looked after the garden and did odd jobs.

Mrs Doyne was not due until Friday, and the kitchen was already showing evidence of Frances' chaotic housekeeping. It would be unkind, and quite wrong, really, to say that Frances was a slut, although, I feel sure, that was Mrs Doyne's private opinion. In some ways, Frances was a very fastidious person. It was just that she never cleared up or put things away where they came from, and seemed quite oblivious to the muddle and mess she created; which was ironic, because when she worked, which wasn't very often, the only jobs she was offered were immaculate young mums in television commercials. In these succinct domestic sagas, her dishes always sparkled like diamonds, her floors were the envy of blowsy neighbours, and you needed polaroids to look at her furniture. Having for a time been married to a genuine, real-life immaculate housewife, I ought to have appreciated Frances' slovenliness more than I did. But there were times when I could cheerfully have strangled her, and in these homicidal moments, it seemed quite incredible that we had been living together for nearly-two years; and I blessed the absconding Frank Fairchild for providing me with free insurance against the peril of marriage. Lately, though, with young mums in the advertisements seeming to get younger every day, Frances had been showing disturbing signs of dissatisfaction with the terms of the policy. She talked on not being prepared to go on like this forever, and wanting to know where she stood.

At least the kitchen was warm. I had banked up the Aga before we had settled down the night before to watch the film, and when I raked out the ashes and opened the flue, it came to life at once. I sat at the battered deal table while Frances, padding about in her bare feet, clutching the blanket with one hand, made the tea.

Gradually, as the warmth seeped into me, I stopped shivering. I felt numbed and curiously detached, and was able quite calmly to tell Frances details of the call from Scotland Yard. She listened in silence. What, after all, could she say? She had only seen my father twice, and all she knew of him was a caricature she must have pieced together from my self-pitying anecdotes. After the way I had neglected him whilst he was alive, she probably thought my outburst of grief at hearing he was dead rather overplayed.

'It's all so bloody incredible,' I said. 'Who in God's name would want to blow up an old man. He was quite harmless.'

'You don't know for certain anyone has,' said Frances, pouring boiling water into the teapot. 'You said the police aren't sure who was in the car.'

'But it was his car,' I said. 'No doubt about that, and they must be pretty certain or they wouldn't ring me up at five in the morning — not a chief superintendent, anyway.'

Frances put a mug of tea in front of me. 'I liked him,' she said reflectively. 'He had violet eyes.'

'Sometimes they looked violet,' I said.

'I was afraid of him, too,' said Frances.

'So was I,' I said. 'I don't know why.'

'What are you going to do?' she said.

'I'll have to go to London . . . identify

the body, I suppose. I'm dreading it.'

She leant over and poured me another cup of tea. 'Do you want some breakfast?' she said.

'God, no!' I said. 'But I'll have some brandy . . . in the tea. That's what he always had . . . after his nightmares.' I could feel myself getting emotional again. I struggled to get a grip on myself while Frances fetched the brandy from the living room. 'What I can't understand,' I said when she came back, 'is what the hell he was doing in Chester Passage at four o'clock in the morning.'

The telephone rang again just as I was raising the mug of fortified tea to my mouth. A jet of scalding liquid slopped out and trickled down my chest.

'I'll go,' said Frances.

'If it's what the Super called the media,' I gasped, 'I'm not here and you don't know anything.'

'I'll say it's a wrong number,' said Frances. 'It's 412 they want.'

The two cats, which had stretched themselves out in the warmest position in front of the stove, pricked up their ears at the sound of the telephone. They got up, arched their backs, and followed Frances into the hall. They hadn't had such an interesting morning since the pigeon flew down the chimney. In a few moments Frances was back.

'It's Dorkes,' she said.

I buried my face in my hands. In all the drama and confusion, I had completely forgotten about Dorkes.

'He keeps calling me 'madam', and he wants to speak to Mister Charles,' said Frances.

'Oh, Christ,' I said. 'I suppose I shall have to talk to him.'

I scarcely recognised Dorkes' voice. The oil had gone out of the Welsh cadences, replaced by a grating anxiety.

'I hope I'm not out of place calling you, Mr Charles,' he said. 'But I'm worried about the Colonel. Is he with you, sir?'

'No,' I said. 'He's not here.'

'I don't quite know what to do,' said Dorkes. 'It's very worrying. He's not at the flat; his bed's not been slept in and the car's gone. The police have been here, sir, asking questions and nosing around.

They won't tell me what it's all about, Mr Charles.'

'Where are you, Mr Dorkes?' I asked.

'I'm at the flat, sir,' he said. 'I came in at half-past five because the Colonel hasn't been sleeping well lately, and he likes his breakfast at six. There were two policemen here, sir.'

'In the flat, do you mean?'

'In the flat, yes. They had the key. I don't know how they got hold of it, but they definitely had the key. The only thing I could think of, Mr Charles, was that he might be with you.'

'Are the police there now?'

'No, sir. They've gone. I thought I'd better let you know, Mr Charles, in case the Colonel . . . well, he's been depressed lately, sir. I hope I did right to call you, sir.'

'Quite right, Mr Dorkes,' I said. 'I'm coming to London this morning. Can you stay at the flat and keep an eye on things until I get there?'

'I was going to stay, sir, in case the Colonel comes back.'

'Thank you, Mr Dorkes,' I said. 'It's

probably all a fuss about nothing.'

'It's not like him, sir,' said Dorkes. 'Not to leave a note or nothing. And what with the police and everything, well, it's very worrying.'

Both cats had jumped on to the table; both cats were trying their best to usurp the little animal I was holding to my ear.

'Just a minute, Mr Dorkes,' I said. I shouted for Frances. 'For Christ's sake come and get these bloody animals off me, will you?'

She came to my rescue. She had discarded the blanket, and now wore jeans and a roll-neck sweater. She dragged the clinging cats from my shoulders, shooed them out and shut the door. Then she perched beside me on the table.

'Look, Mr Dorkes,' I resumed. 'I'll be up there as soon as I possibly can. We'll just have to hope for the best.'

I put the receiver down. Frances swept the hair out of her eyes and gazed at me enquiringly. 'What now?' she said.

'It's getting a bloody sight worse all the time,' I said. 'Dorkes got to the flat at half-past five and found the police had let themselves in. They'd got hold of the key from somewhere. The old man had disappeared and so had the car.'

'Doesn't he know about the bomb?' said Frances.

'Apparently not. The Police didn't tell him anything. He thought my father might be here.'

'Do you want a bath?' said Frances. 'The water should be hot by now.'

'Yes,' I said. 'And then I'll have to go. Shove some things in a bag for me, will you? Christ! I don't know when I felt so ghastly.'

'What things?' she said.

'Shirts, pants . . . you know,' I said. 'God knows how long all this is going to take. I don't suppose I shall get back tonight.' I started on my way to the bathroom, which was a converted outhouse leading off the kitchen in contravention of any number of bye-laws. 'I'll phone you as soon as I know,' I added over my shoulder.

'You won't,' said Frances. 'I'm coming too.'

I stopped in my tracks and turned to face her. 'There's no point in you coming,' I said.

'I'm not stopping here by myself.'

'No need for you to get involved,' I said.

'Hurry up and have that bath,' she said. 'I'm coming.'

'Frances,' I pleaded. 'Darling . . . I'd much rather you stayed here and looked after things. We can't both walk out and leave the cats.'

'Why don't you want me?' she demanded.

'It's not that,' I lied, and then, unwisely, added: 'Things are complicated enough.'

'And I'd make them worse? OK. Go on your own.'

'Please!' I said. 'Please, don't make things difficult.'

The water wasn't really hot, and it came out of the ancient brass tap in a turgid, brownish trickle. I felt guilty about Frances, but I knew I had to keep her out of it. I didn't feel capable of coping with her as well as all the rest. I shouldn't have said it, but she did complicate things. I was afraid she would either start a row or sulk; but when I emerged from the bathroom, she seemed to have accepted my prohibition. At any rate, she didn't mention coming with me again, and was putting on a show of brisk efficiency. She might have been a dutiful wife seeing her hubby off on a business trip.

'I've put in three pairs of pants,' she said. 'I know what you're like. If you want any soap, you'll have to buy some when you get there. Have you got enough money?'

'For the moment.'

'Petrol?'

'I think so, it'll get me to the A.11.'

'Handkerchief?'

'Yes, yes. You'll be all right?'

'Me? I'll be all right. I'm going back to bed and staying there.'

She came with me to the front door. I kissed her, and for a moment she clung to me.

'Sorry,' she said. 'Sorry, and all that.'

4

The Morgan was garaged in what had once been stabling but now was a ruin. The roof timbers were rotten and liable to collapse at any moment. They were entitled to collapse, according to Dad Doyne. There was no nature, he said, left in them. The local builder had been to look at it months ago. He had said all that was holding it up were the old swallows' nests. He promised to see what he could do, but so far he hadn't come back. I doubted if he ever would.

I knew it was absurd to have a Morgan. I wasn't the Morgan type, I would have loved to have been, but I wasn't. I knew I ought to sell it before the roof fell and crushed it, but somehow, although it was uncomfortable, draughty and scared me to death, I couldn't bring myself to part with it. Frances said it compensated for my sexual inadequacy, but when I asked her whether that was a complaint, she said, no, it was a comment. Actually, she may have been right, in a way. I bought my first sports car shortly after my divorce, although whether it was a feeling of inadequacy or relief which prompted the indulgence, it would be hard to say.

My father had been dead against my marriage, and on this occasion, my mother took his side. They said we were both too young; but what they meant was that Helen was not of the Rowlands' class. It was a terrible blow to them when Helen's tearful claims to pregnancy induced me to defy them, and we were married secretly at a Registry Office. She wasn't pregnant, of course, and once married, devoted herself with clinical single-mindedness to avoiding becoming so.

After my father cut his wrist and was spending a second spell in the Hampstead clinic, my mother and I moved back to Chelsea. When he came out we stayed on in London. This time the treatment seemed to have achieved an astonishing success. It was as though a heavy burden had been lifted from him and life had taken on a new meaning. He even started to work in an import/export agency, run, so he said, by a man he had known in the war. I never actually met this shadowy figure, and I never discovered exactly what was imported or exported, nor where the firm had its offices. I gathered they were somewhere near London Bridge. It was a rather vague job, but it was certainly not a sinecure. It involved work at curious hours and a good deal of travelling abroad. I didn't really take much interest; it was enough for me that my father seemed to be cured and was out of the way a lot of the time.

My mother, too, was delighted to be back in the centre of things, surrounded by people, traffic and buildings, and once again able to plunge into the social whirl.

Having got my way about the Slade, I, too, was happy for a while. Then a gradual disillusionment set in. A niggling doubt haunted me that perhaps my talent was not quite so extraordinary as I and my mother had believed. It was a doubt which seemed to be shared by the teaching staff, who were always extolling the advantages of a career in commercial art. This, I assumed, was their kindly way of telling me I was good for nothing else.

When I left the Slade I got a job with a small advertising agency, and it was here that I met Helen, a blonde, doll-like typist who lived with a widowed mother in Surbiton. She was nineteen and I was twenty-three, and after our clandestine marriage we set up house in a tiny flat in Maida Vale. For a long time my father refused to speak to me, and I had to meet my mother either when he was away, or furtively at Harrods. I think my mother might have been prepared to make the best of a bad job; but it was Helen who displayed an unsuspected streak of either pride or obstinacy and refused be made the best of. She said I was a 'mother's boy', and should stand on my own two feet. I didn't tell her about the cheques my mother slipped into my pocket when we met, which were paying for the flat; and I hadn't the courage to say I was fed up in those pre-pill days, with douches, Dutch caps and calendars.

I had been married a year when my

Italian grandfather died and my mother came into her inheritance. Bureaucratic and legal complications made it sensible for both my parents to move to Rome, where, conveniently, it seemed, my father could continue his import/export activities. I used to visit them twice a year. Helen did not come with me, and in my absence, as I was to discover later, she did not waste time pining for her hubby. One night I came back from Rome to find that she had flown our nest in Maida Vale and gone to live with a middle-aged property developer in Rickmansworth.

She wrote me an absurd letter, accusing me of a whole catalogue of marital crimes, and imploring me to give her what she called her 'freedom', as though I had been keeping her in duress vile.

The divorce proceedings were protracted, painful and expensive, and I suppose it was a refuge from the sordid complications of adult life that I began to write and illustrate books for young children. After a number of false starts I achieved a modest success with my

Porker Family series. The money I made wasn't enough to live on, and I continued to work at the agency until in 1976 my mother suffered a fatal brain haemorrhage, and I in my turn came into the Italian money.

In my innocence I imagined that in weeks, or at the most a few months, large sums would be at my disposal. In reality, I came up against all the delays and obstructions that had compelled my parents to take up residence in Italy. On the strength of my prospects, however, the bank lent me the money to buy Duck End Farmhouse, and I threw up the agency job and retired into rural solitude.

I suppose people thought I was queer in a number of senses; a man of thirty-two, living alone, apart from two cats, and with no occupation other than drawing pictures of funny pigs. But after my traumatic experience of marriage to Helen, I was determined not to get seriously involved with another woman, which was why when I woke up and found Frances beside me, I couldn't quite understand how it happened. I wasn't clear, either, and this was more serious, where it would end.

For a driver in my exhausted state, the Morgan had one advantage at least. That was that it was almost impossible to doze off at the wheel. In a car with an efficient heater, no force ten gale whipping through gaps in the hood or a suspension that had apparently been constructed out of granite, I would probably have dropped off after a few miles. As it was, the freezing wind, the spine jarring, and the precarious power of the noisy engine, kept me awake and the adrenalin flowing.

It was seven o'clock when I reached Stowmarket and the main A.11 road. I slowed down and switched on the radio. It was essential to slow down, because at speeds over twenty the noise blotted out every other sound. I was just in time for the news bulletin. There was something about Rhodesia; a strike at Leyland; the Chinese had done something which had annoyed the Russians; the balance of payments was appalling. And then . . . a car bomb in London. I dropped down to a crawl and fiddled with the volume control.

'Early this morning,' said the girl newsreader, 'a bomb planted in a parked car went off in the Bloomsbury area of London. Following the explosion the car burst into flames and was almost completely gutted. One man is known to have been killed, and considerable damage was caused over a wide area. There is an unconfirmed report from Dublin that the IRA have claimed responsibility in a telephone call to the Irish Times. The dead man has not yet been identified, but it is known that the car, a 1940 Rover saloon was registered in the name of Colonel Vivien Rowlands. Colonel Rowlands was one of the British Special Operations officers to be dropped by parachute into Yugoslavia during the last war. He fought with the Communist Partisans, was awarded the DSO and became a personal friend of Marshal Tito. For many years he lived in Italy. The police are concerned that this latest outrage may be the start of a renewed wave of IRA terrorism directed at mainland targets. And now . . . football. In the second round of the European Cup Winners Cup, Nottingham Forest . . . '

I switched the radio off. They hadn't said my father was dead in so many words, but, despite the awkward juggling with past and present tenses, the implication was obvious. It was a weird sensation, hearing that potted biography — or was it an obituary? — and it triggered off a flood of memories, going back to my earliest childhood. I remembered the DSO which I had swopped for a Dinky toy, and the precious book, Djalas's 'Life of Tito', inscribed on the flyleaf, in what I was told was the Marshal's own hand: 'To Vivian, hero of Kjanek and the bravest of comrades. Josip.' I remembered vividly, too, my first day at school, when another five year old freshman had said: 'My dad's a doctor — what's yours?', and I replied 'My dad's the hero of Kjanek.'

I didn't know what it meant, but it sounded grander than a doctor. I discovered later that Kjanek was a mountain in Montenegro, notorious in the history of the Yugoslav conflict for the massacre which had taken place there. Over two hundred men, women and children, who had taken refuge in the caves, were slaughtered by the Germans. My father had been the sole survivor, left for dead beneath a pile of mangled corpses.

When my father returned to England after my mother's death, he had taken a lease on a flat in Vernon Mews, Chelsea. He lived alone, a reclusive existence, and although the old Rover had been brought out of storage, he rarely used it or ventured further than the Imperial Services Club off St James' Square. He did not seem to have any intimate friends, and if he entertained, it was usually for lunch at the club.

The Imperial Services Club was an obscure institution, a sombre, Victorian mausoleum. It had been founded during the Boer War, and a forbidding, gimlet-eyed picture of the Old Queen dominated the entrance hall. The massive furniture was shabby, the servants servile and decrepit, and the members mostly retired army officers. The place depressed me, and made me edgy. I felt I had no right to be there, an opinion the majority of members clearly shared.

The club's porter was an ex-sergeant major called Pond. He had a bulbous nose and little fierce red eyes. His uniform was a top hat and a blue knee-length coat with silver buttons. The first time I went to the club, my father introduced me.

'Mr Pond,' he said, 'this is my son, Charles.'

Pond stiffened up, as though coming to attention. His sad, lined, leathery face underwent an extraordinary transformation. It seemed to light up with devotion, almost with adoration. He beamed at me.

'Very pleased to make your acquaintance, sir,' he said.

I hesitated, not knowing how I was expected to behave. Would shaking hands with the porter be a gross breach of club etiquette; would failure to do so appear offensive? I held out my hand, hoping I was doing the right thing. It seemed I was.

'A chip off the old block, Colonel,' said Pond, turning his worshipping gaze back on my father.

They stood chatting for a few minutes, ignoring me. Members in various stages of senility passed through the hall, eyeing us curiously, asking about letters or messages, demanding taxis. I noticed that they called the porter 'George' and he addressed them as 'sir'. Only my father, it seemed, dignified him as Mr Pond, and only my father was accorded his rank by Pond. Clearly there was a special relationship between them, not shared by other members.

'Pond is a good fellow,' said my father as we ate our lamb cutlets in the gloomy dining-room. 'Eighth Army and then all through the Italian campaign. Wounded at Monte Cassino. Came across him when I was in dock over there. Actually I went to his wedding. Married an Italian girl.'

'Like you,' I said.

My father looked surprised, and then puzzled. Evidently he found it hard to make the connection.

'Local girl,' he said. 'Father was a baker, I seem to recall.'

I wasn't interested in Pond or his life history, but at least it was conversation, and filled what would otherwise have been long, awkward silences. To keep it going, I said, 'Any children?'

'Dispersed,' said my father.

The word seemed farcically inappropriate, and in trying to suppress an involuntary laugh, I choked on a piece of mutton, attracting disagreeable glares from other tables.

'Can't speak a word of English,' said my father when I had recovered.

'Who?'

'Pond's wife.'

'Oh,' I said. Was this the reason the Pond offspring had dispersed? 'I imagine that must be rather awkward.'

'Not necessarily,' said my father.

Some months later, on another lunchtime appointment with my father at the club, Pond wasn't there. In his place was another porter who, apart from the top hat, bore a striking resemblance to Hitler.

'Where's Mr Pond?' I asked my father.

This time we were eating braised sheeps' hearts.

'Retired,' said my father. 'Didn't I tell you? They've gone to live in Italy. Wife was never happy here. Can't speak a word of English.'

'You did tell me that,' I said.

'I helped them find a little farm not far from Rome. Well, a smallholding, really — nothing much — goats and that sort of thing.'

'You mean you helped them financially?' I asked.

'I did what I could,' he said. 'Not easy now-a-days, taxes and one thing and another.'

'Really, father,' I said. 'Was that wise?'

'An investment, in a way,' he said. 'I can always go there if things get tiresome . . .'

He broke off, fixing me with his curious, violet eyes, too delicate and innocent for their rugged setting. They seemed to belong to another, softer face. His eyes seemed to be appealing to me; the mute plea of a woman or a child demanding the impossible — to be loved for ever, to be given a slice of the moon.

'Can you understand that, old chap?' he asked.

'Of course,' I said. 'We all feel like getting away from it all, sometimes.'

'I want you to understand,' he said.

I didn't know what he was talking about, but I thought it best to humour him. 'I can't picture you as a goat-herd,' I said. 'You wouldn't like it for long.'

'It wouldn't be for long,' he said. 'Nothing's for very long at my age.'

I wanted to ask how much the little help he had given Pond amounted to, but I hadn't the nerve. His eccentric philanthropy dismayed me. I didn't want him to get involved with another unsavoury ex-soldier like Edwin Dorkes, but I knew that if I remonstrated with him, not only would it do no good, but my motives would almost certainly be misconstrued.

My father relapsed into gloomy introspection which lasted until we had finished our rhubarb and custard and were drinking coffee in the ante-room. Suddenly he let out a short, barking laugh.

'Goat-herd!' he said. 'I must tell Edwin that; I think it will amuse him.'

'I didn't think Edwin had much sense of humour,' I said.

My father considered this. 'No?' he said. 'Well, perhaps not a sense of humour, exactly, but he has a great sense of fun.'

Applied to a man who had murdered two people and very nearly murdered a third, 'fun' seemed another singularly inappropriate choice of word.

I had not been aware of the existence of Pond before my father introduced him that day at the club; but I had been aware of Edwin Dorkes all my life. Occasionally my mother had made oblique references, which I did not understand, to a poor woman with a little boy about my own age, whom Daddy helped in her misfortunes. My father never referred to the subject at all, until I was grown up. Then I discovered that the poor woman was the widow of the wireless operator killed on the blind drop into Yugoslavia, and that Edwin was his son, six months old when his father died.

I suppose my father felt responsible in some way for the soldier's death; guilty, even. Perhaps that was just me, because I was so selfish I couldn't conceive that my father's altruism could be as pure as it seemed. Apart from the financial help he gave them — I had no idea on what scale — he took a more than casual interest in Edwin's progress and career. Encouraged by my father, Edwin joined the army when he was sixteen as an Apprentice Artificer. I gathered he took to the life like a duck to water, came top of his course, was a sergeant by the time he was twenty, and soon afterwards was selected for the elite, hard-men corps, the SAS.

This promising military career came to an abrupt end in Northern Ireland.

For a time — I surmised this because the Army doesn't admit to such irregular activities — he was employed on under cover work in the Republic. Whether this was so or not, he was certainly dressed as a civilian on the evening he shot and killed two citizens of Eire outside a pub in a remote border area. The Irish Government made a great fuss, but the Army whisked Dorkes out of the way, back to the mainland, and, while offering to co-operate with the Guarda in every possible way, steadfastly maintained that none of their men were, or could possibly have been, responsible.

The Army got shot of Dorkes hurriedly, a tame psychiatrist certifying him as emotionally unstable. Discharged on medical grounds, he drifted about working as an electrician on building sites, and then got a job as a so-called Security Officer in a gaming club near Victoria Station. This came to another abrupt and violent end when, in a brawl, he very nearly killed an elderly punter. For this he was sentenced to two years for GBH.

All this happened whilst my father was living in Italy. When he came back, Dorkes was in Wandsworth prison, with a year of his sentence still to run. My father went to his rescue, pulled all the strings he could, and as a result Dorkes was paroled within a few weeks. I suppose my father undertook to act as a sort of guardian. In any event, he set Dorkes up as an electrical contractor in Fulham, and in return, Dorkes acted as part-time batman. Nearly every morning, he rode over to Chelsea on his motor-bike, got my father's breakfast, did whatever shopping was required, cleaned up, and drove the old Rover if my father wanted to go anywhere. The rest of his time, he mended fridges, washing machines and vacuum cleaners, in Fulham.

The peculiar thing about Edwin Dorkes, or one of them, was that he didn't look the violent type. Outwardly, at any rate, he was quite the reverse. He was a shortish, sharp-featured man, with a diffident manner and a soft, Welsh voice. He was always polite and neatly dressed, his shoes polished to a glass-like finish, his wavy black hair and his guards type moustache trim and immaculate. Only his hands belied his otherwise mild and harmless appearance. They were large, square, powerful hands, given a macabre touch by the absence on the left of a little finger.

'Wonderful with his hands,' I remembered my father saying. 'Do anything with his hands. Born mechanic — he's made the Rover good as new — splendid job. Electrical, too! Edwin understands it all. Tricky, fiddling little jobs — quite amazing. Great pity he lost that finger.'

I detested Dorkes. I should have been grateful for the apparent devotion with which he looked after my father, relieving me of that responsibility, but I distrusted him and suspected his motives. Deep down, I suppose, I resented him, and was jealous of his closeness to my father, and I always translated praise for Dorkes into implied criticism of my own uselessness. I also had the uneasy feeling that beneath the veneer of respect and his ingratiating manner — he always called me Mister Charles — he despised me and my way of life. What his own private life was like, I had no idea, but I gathered from my father's eulogies that it was of a puritanical rectitude. This made me distrust him even more deeply. I always distrust puritans; they usually turn out to be perverts of some sort.

5

I reached London at the height of the morning traffic chaos, and it was nearly eleven by the time I found my way to New Scotland Yard. I was surprised how normal everything seemed — no guns, no screaming sirens, and in the headquarters of the Metropolitan Police, an atmosphere of phlegmatic calm.

I had never been to Scotland Yard, and my mental image of what it would be like had been derived from watching venerable British films. I expected Victorian fustiness; dim corridors along which cockney constables plodded bearing cups of tea for the Guv'nor, who sat smoking a pipe in a cluttered office, with shabby furniture, grimy windows and a coal fire. In one corner, inevitably, there would be an antique stand for trilbys and mackintoshes.

When I discovered that Scotland Yard was now housed in a modern building of concrete and glass, with carpets, airline chairs and potted plants, I felt as let down as if I had arrived at 221B Baker Street, to find that it had been replaced by a boutique.

A young WPC, as toothy and hygienic as a Pan-Am hostess, flew me by high speed lift to the sixth floor, where, in a bright uncluttered executive-type office, I met Chief Superintendent Barker. My preconceptions suffered another reverse, for Barker was not in the least as I had imagined him. I had met men like Barker in publishers' offices; smooth, middle-aged trendies, with artificially curled grey hair and clothes a fraction too obviously expensive. His handshake was so warm and his expression so sincere, that I thought for a moment he was going to tell me that although, personally, he loved my work, it did not quite fit the firm's list.

'Good of you to come so promptly, Mr Rowlands,' he said.

'I'm afraid I'm rather late,' I said stupidly. 'The traffic . . . '

'I know,' his voice vibrated with sympathy. 'I know. What is the answer? Is there an answer?'

An internal door opened and another man came into the room. He, at least, was reassuringly true to type. Bulky, balding, with a ruddy face, off the peg suit and massive, square-toed shoes.

'Ah . . . John . . . ' Barker greeted him. 'This is Mr Rowlands . . . the . . . er . . . the son.' He turned to me. 'Chief Inspector Claydon,' he explained. 'The Chief Inspector is in charge of anti-terrorist operations.'

Claydon gave me a wary, critical look. He muttered,

'Good morning', but he did not shake hands.

'Please sit down,' said Barker.

I took a tubular metal chair facing Barker; Claydon sat at the side of the desk.

'I'm sure all this has come as a great shock to you, Mr Rowlands,' said Barker.

'It's unbelievable,' I said. 'I didn't believe it, actually, until I heard the news on the car radio . . . '

'Ah!' Barker held up his hand deprecatingly. 'That was rather naughty of the

Beeb. I'm afraid they jumped the gun, implying that Colonel Rowlands . . . I don't know how they ferreted out the bit about the car; we've certainly released nothing officially to the media.'

'But it *was* his car?' I said.

'Oh, yes,' said Barker. 'It was his car.'

'Please,' I pleaded. 'I'm very confused. Was it my father who was killed or not? I'd like to know.'

Barker turned to Claydon, who pinched his nose and cleared his throat.

'That is our working theory, sir,' he said. 'The evidence is circumstantial; there has been no positive identification.'

'I suppose,' I said hesitantly, 'I suppose you want me to identify the body.'

Barker and Claydon exchanged glances. 'Normally that would be the procedure, sir,' he said.

'We don't wish to cause you needless distress,' said Barker.

I found it difficult to speak; my mouth was dry and there was a hard lump stuck in my throat.

'We estimate something in the region of ten pounds of explosive was used,' said

Claydon. 'That's a lot of explosive in a confined space like a car. Then there was this petrol. Apart from what was in the tank there are indications that there were a number of full cans in the back. Possibly five or six gallons.'

'By the time the fire brigade arrived,' said Barker, 'there was . . . well, there was considerable fire damage.'

'You mean,' I managed to croak, 'You mean identification isn't possible?'

'There is a problem, sir,' said Claydon.

'Do you mind if I smoke?' I said.

'Of course,' said Barker. 'Of course.' But it was Claydon who brought a packet out of his pocket and held it out to me.

'But surely . . . ' I said. 'I thought . . . the teeth . . . '

'We are talking about this early stage in the investigation,' said Barker. 'Forensic examination takes time.'

'Teeth aren't much help without a complete dental record,' said Claydon. 'This may be difficult to trace. Colonel Rowlands lived abroad, didn't he, sir?'

'He was in Italy for about ten years,' I

said. 'My parents went there in 1967, I think it was.'

'1968, actually,' said Barker.

'Probably,' I said. 'I'm not very good at dates.'

'At the moment,' said Barker, 'a number of things suggest that the dead man was Colonel Rowlands. We know it was his car; we know he's missing, and then there are some personal items salvaged from the wreckage. I'd like you to look at them, sir.'

He opened a drawer and brought about a large box file. From it he took out a signet ring, a pocket watch, a bunch of keys, and finally, making my stomach heave, a charred shoe.

'These keys belong to his flat,' he said, 'and the shoe was made by Dawson's in Jermyn Street. They confirm the Colonel was one of their customers, although, of course, they can't say definitely that this particular shoe was his. Then there's this watch.'

'It looks like my father's,' I said.

'There's an inscription inside the lid,' said Barker. 'In a foreign language.'

'Serbo-Croat,' I said.

'That is so,' said Barker. 'We've had it translated. The watch appears to be a presentation from the People's Republic of Yugoslavia.'

'Yes,' I said. 'He fought with them during the war. I suppose you know all about that. They made him a sort of National hero.' I laughed a trifle hysterically. 'It's ironic, really, because he was violently anti-communist.'

'Well,' said Barker, 'didn't Shakespeare say that war makes strange bedfellows, or something of the sort.'

'I thought that was misery,' I said.

There was a knock on the door and another toothy WPC came in bearing a tray with three cups.

'Ah!' Barker rubbed his hands and beamed at her. 'Thank you, Mary. You'll have some coffee, Mr Rowlands — or would you prefer tea?'

'Thank you,' I said. 'I'd love a cup of coffee.'

'I think we all need it,' said Barker. 'It's been a hard morning.'

The coffee was remarkably good, and

for some time we concentrated upon it in silence. The noise of the traffic outside came muffled through the double glazing; telephones could be heard ringing in other parts of the building, and then, as though from a great distance, Big Ben tolled the half hour.

'Would you mind putting that shoe away,' I said.

'So sorry,' said Barker. 'Of course . . . ' He returned all the exhibits to the box. 'We shall have to keep these for the time being. But, they will be handed to you or your father's legal representative in due course. I assume you are the next of kin?'

'I suppose I must be,' I said. 'My mother's dead and I'm an only child. The only other close relative I know about is an uncle. He lives in Kenya.'

'I don't know about these keys,' said Barker. 'You may need them.'

'I think my father's . . . well, his sort of man-servant . . . has a set,' I said.

'Ah, yes!' said Barker. 'Ah, yes. This fellow Dorkes.'

There was another silence while we finished our coffee.

'It would help us if you could tell us something about your father,' said Claydon, placing his empty cup carefully on the edge of the desk. 'Interests, friends, activities, and so on. If someone went to this trouble to kill him, there must have been a good reason.'

'I can't imagine why anyone should want to kill him,' I said. 'The only thing I can think of is that it was a ghastly mistake. Whoever did it thought someone else was in the car. It's happened before, hasn't it?'

'A possibility,' said Barker. 'But rather remote in this case, I should say. Why, for instance, was the car in Chester Passage at that time in the morning?'

'A blind alley,' put in Claydon. 'Lock up garages on one side and a blank wall on the other.'

'He must have gone there deliberately,' said Barker. 'Perhaps to meet someone. Have you any idea who that someone might have been?'

'It's not the sort of place you end up in by chance,' added Claydon.

The way they were orchestrating, and

the increasing tempo of their voices, gave me the unpleasant sensation that I was a suspect under interrogation. I wanted to shout: 'I didn't do it!', but I wasn't sure that I hadn't done it, indirectly. I tried not to look as guilty as I felt.

'I've rather been out of touch with him lately,' I said lamely. 'I only saw him very occasionally. As far as I know he lived very quietly. I don't think he had any close friends, just acquaintances at the club . . . that sort of thing.'

'Curious time,' said Claydon. 'Curious time for an elderly gentleman to be driving round Bloomsbury and parking up a blind alley.'

'That's another thing I can't understand,' I said. 'He never drove at night. If he wanted to go anywhere he either took a taxi, or Dorkes would drive.'

'Oh, Dorkes would drive, would he?' said Barker.

'You said your mother died some years ago,' said Claydon.

'Did I,' I said. 'Well, yes, its perfectly true. About three years ago . . . that's when my father came back to England.'

'Any lady friends?' said Claydon.

'Very unlikely,' I said. 'He was a bit past that sort of thing.'

'Early sixties,' said Claydon. 'Not all that old by today's standards.'

'He wasn't the type,' I said.

'What type's that, sir?' said Claydon.

'This chap Dorkes,' Barker intervened abruptly. He had a blue covered folder open on the desk in front of him. 'Tell me what you know about him.'

'A sort of part-time valet, chauffeur and housemaid,' I said.

'He was a regular soldier, I see,' said Barker. 'Criminal record. From what you've told me I shouldn't have thought he was exactly your father's cup of tea.'

'It's all a bit complicated,' I said, and tried to explain about Sergeant Dorkes who had been killed on the blind drop, and my father's relationship with the widow and her son. Barker listened in silence. When I had finished he turned to Claydon.

'Curious he should have been in the SAS,' he said. 'Don't you think that curious?'

Claydon shrugged, and before he could answer, I rushed in.

'They could have thought Dorkes was in the car,' I said. 'It makes sense that the IRA would be out to get him after what happened in Northern Ireland.'

'If it was the IRA,' said Barker.

'But on the News,' I said. 'Didn't the IRA phone the Irish Times and say they'd done it?'

'Someone phoned,' said Claydon. 'They even gave an IRA authenticating codeword.'

'The only trouble is,' said Barker, 'it was several years out of date.'

'I'm afraid you've lost me,' I said.

'The security forces in Northern Ireland have this arrangement with the IRA,' said Barker. 'Genuine IRA messages are always authenticated by a prearranged codeword, changed every few months.'

'They could have made a mistake,' I said. 'Used an out of date codeword.'

'And blown up the wrong man?' said Barker. 'Too much of a coincidence.'

'They don't make that sort of mistake,'

said Claydon. 'One thing you can say about the bastards — they're reliable. They're honest, too, if you can apply that word to murderers. They never claim responsibility for something they didn't do, like a lot of terrorists' gangs.'

'You think that's what happened?' I asked. 'Whoever did it is trying to put the blame on the IRA?'

'It's possible,' Barker answered for him. 'We simply don't know.'

'But we intend to find out!' Claydon burst out with a sudden show of anger. His complexion turned a darker shade of red. 'Bloody foreigners! I'm sick of the sight of them. Fanatics, creeps and crackpots from all over the world; London attracts them like a bloody magnet. And we let them in; we hand out Social Security and give the women free abortions . . .'

'That's political, John,' interrupted Barker reprovingly.

Claydon subsided. 'If you say so, Chief,' he said.

'Wasn't your father in the Foreign Office?' asked Barker.

'Oh, years and years ago,' I said. 'He had to leave . . . because of his health.'

Barker pursed his lips and nodded sympathetically. 'Ah,' he said.

'He had . . . a nervous breakdown,' I said. 'His nerves were pretty badly affected by what he went through in the war.'

'Understandable,' said Barker. 'Didn't he have some business interests?'

'He had some sort of connection with a city company,' I said. 'Import/export, I think. I never knew much about it.'

Once again Barker turned to Claydon. 'Might be worth following that one up, John,' he said. Then, to me: 'What are your plans, Mr Rowlands?'

'I haven't made any plans,' I said. 'What's going to happen now? Will there be an inquest or something?'

'There will have to be an inquest,' said Barker. 'I expect under the circumstances the Coroner will decide to adjourn a formal hearing until we have completed our investigations. We'll let you know. Will you be going straight back to Suffolk?'

'I don't really know,' I said. 'I expect I

shall stay at the flat to-night, at any rate. My father may turn up.'

'He may, indeed,' said Barker. 'He may, indeed. But I shouldn't count on it, Mr Rowlands.'

6

Big Ben was booming mid-day as I left Scotland Yard and drove along Victoria Street towards Chelsea. An icy drizzle was falling from a forlorn grey sky, and the lights already burning in the offices and shops seemed to deepen rather than relieve the pervading gloom. I thought: what a bloody awful day for the hero of Kjanek to get himself blown up. And then, something that had been niggling at the back of my mind ever since Barker's five o'clock 'phone call, came to the surface. Kjanek. Yugoslavia. Could there be a connection between the violence that had erupted that morning in a Bloomsbury alleyway, and those barbaric events in the Balkan mountains, so far away both in distance and time?

I told myself that the idea was ridiculous. All that after all, was now ancient history. But I couldn't quite get rid of the feeling that there was a connection.

Outside Victoria Station the first editions of the evening papers were on the stands. I glimpsed a poster: 'London Car Bomb. Latest,' before I was engulfed in the turmoil of traffic trying to get in and out of the station forecourt.

Vernon Mews was off Vernon Square, a quiet back-water of large Victorian houses which were now converted into flats or used as offices by obscure societies and minor embassies. At the entrance to the Mews there was a notice 'Private Property. No Unauthorised Parking.' The cobbled courtyard was deserted, the drizzle had turned to sleet, and the aura of desolation came as an anti-climax. I had half-expected the place to be thronged with police, reporters, television crews and morbid sightseers. The absence of interest seemed painfully pathetic, but with so much death and destruction going on in the world, there was no logical reason why anyone should bother to stand about in the icy rain because one, unimportant old man had been wiped out by a bomb eight hours ago. Thousands, millions, perhaps, had died; bombed, shot, starved and battered since four o'clock that morning. If it hadn't been my father, would I have cared?

The Mews was a two storey block of converted stables divided into three flats with garages at ground level and living accommodation above. They were tarted up with insubstantial iron balconies and coaching lamps. When I had asked my father, once, what his neighbours were like, his expression had assumed that trapped look which it always did when he was questioned about his personal affairs. In the end, he had shrugged and said they were 'quiet'. One, I knew was a retired Civil Servant, and the other Lady Somebody-or-other who only used the flat during what she still fondly believed was the London season.

My father's flat was in the middle; I rang the bell and, after a long interval, there was the scrabbling sound of a chain being removed, and the front door opened marginally to reveal Dorkes' anxious face.

'Hello, Mr Dorkes,' I said.

He opened the door, glancing over his shoulder as he did so, a mannerism of his, as though he were constantly expecting an attack from the rear.

'What a terrible thing, Mr Charles,' he said, hushed and funereal. 'I don't know what to say, I don't, honestly.'

He stood back to let me into the tiny hallway, and, as I brushed past him, I could smell distinctly the fumes of whisky carried on his breath.

'Thank God you're here, sir,' he said.

He led the way up the stairs and ushered me through a door on the landing into another minute hall.

'Let me take your coat, sir,' he said. 'What weather!'

He took my sheepskin coat, and gave it a little shake before hanging it up on one of the wall hooks beside my father's Burberry.

The living room with its plain green carpet, Liberty prints and reproduction furniture had the air of a showroom, unlived in and unloved. There was an almost total absence of ornaments or

71

knick-knacks, and the sole personal touch was a row of photographs in silver frames on top of the mock Georgian bureau. There was one of myself, taken when I was a boy — fourteen, I think I'd been — with a rather sickly simper on my face. Beside it was a portrait of my mother taken about the same time, her big, sad eyes gazing out as they had done so often in her life, as though she couldn't quite understand; puzzled and a little anxious. Then there was Churchill, and next to him the round, benevolent looking face of Marshal Tito.

'When I heard the news,' said Dorkes, 'I felt as though I'd been hit with a twelve pound hammer. What a terrible thing, Mr Charles. Terrible. I come in this morning like I told you on the phone and found two coppers here. They didn't say nothing about a bomb. Naturally I thought there'd been an accident. The only thing I could think of was to 'phone you right away.'

'I'm glad you did, Mr Dorkes,' I said.

'It doesn't make sense,' said Dorkes. 'A gentleman like the Colonel. What harm had he ever done anyone?'

'I know,' I said. 'It doesn't make sense. But it's not definite that it was him in the car. I've been to Scotland Yard. They can't say positively who it was.'

'Then where is he?' said Dorkes. 'If it wasn't him, where is he? And it was the Rover, wasn't it? They gave out it was the Rover.'

'I know,' I said. 'It looks bad.'

I slumped into one of the easy chairs. I couldn't remember ever having felt quite so tired.

'When did you see him last?' I said.

'Monday,' said Dorkes. 'I didn't come in Tuesday, because I had this dishwasher to fix out at Balham. He said he'd be OK; he'd spend the day at the club. But I was in Monday first thing and got him his breakfast, and did a bit of shopping.'

'You said on the 'phone he was depressed.'

'Well,' said Dorkes. 'You know what he was like, sir. He had his ups and downs. He wasn't sleeping, that was the real trouble. I tried to get him to take some pills, but he wouldn't. He was dead against pills.'

'Apart from not sleeping too well,' I said, 'did he seem more or less normal?'

'They've asked me that,' said Dorkes. 'The police . . . but what can I say? I didn't notice nothing unusual. What puzzles me is what he was doing out in the car at that time. He never drove himself at night. I haven't the nerve for it, Edwin, he'd say. But I feel safe with you at the wheel. Well, when you've driven over there with bloody snipers taking pot shots at you, and kids round every corner waiting to heave coke bottles full of acid at you through the windscreen, London traffic's a picnic. You look all in, Mr Charles. Can I get you some coffee?'

'I could do with a drink,' I said.

'There's not a drop in the place, sir,' said Dorkes solemnly. 'You know the Colonel didn't hold with it . . . except a little wine with a meal. Never touch the stuff myself, sir. Never have done. Wouldn't know what it tastes like.'

I tried to hide my incredulity. 'Isn't there some brandy or something?' I said.

'My father always used to have some brandy in his tea when . . . well, when he couldn't sleep.'

'We did have a little brandy,' admitted Dorkes. 'For emergencies, like you say.'

'Well,' I said. 'If this isn't an emergency, I don't know what is.'

'We're right out,' said Dorkes. 'I had it down on my list for to-day. But I can go out and get something for you, if you like, sir.'

'Don't bother,' I said. 'I'll have some coffee, then, if it's not too much trouble.'

'It's no trouble,' said Dorkes. 'No trouble at all, Mr Charles.'

I followed him into the tiny kitchen where everything was meticulously neat, the chrome fittings gleaming and the formica spotless. It looked as thought it had just been made ready for the CO's inspection. Even the precisely folded washing up towels looked as though they had been ironed. I found the sterility of it all depressing, and I thought with nostalgia of the muck and muddle of the kitchen at Duck End. Dorkes set about making the coffee as though it were a military exercise, and I sensed that he resented my intrusion into a restricted area.

'Do the Police know who done it?' he asked.

'No,' I said. 'The only thing I gathered was that they don't think it was the IRA.'

Dorkes gave a derisive snort. 'It was the IRA all right!' he said. 'I know the bastards. Hanging's too good for them — they want castrating.'

'They wouldn't have any reason to kill my father,' I said.

'Reason!' he said. 'Reason don't come into it, Mr Charles. They're like animals; they don't reason. Anyway, they've admitted it haven't they? It was on the News.'

'The police don't think the message was genuine,' I said. 'The codeword was out of date or something.'

Dorkes didn't answer. He arranged the cups carefully on a tray. 'I'll bring it into the other room,' he said. 'Codeword?' he said, when I was settled in an easy chair drinking the coffee. 'They don't know what they're talking about.'

'I only know what they told me,' I said. 'They seem to think my father went to meet someone.'

'In the middle of the night?' said Dorkes. 'Who would he meet in the middle of the night?'

'Could have been a woman, I suppose,' I said.

'The police said that?' He was outraged. 'That's just the way their dirty minds work. That's all they can think of — dirt.'

'Well, it's not unreasonable,' I said. 'After all, my mother's been dead a long time now.'

'I should have thought you'd have known your dad better than that,' he said severely.

'I don't think it's likely,' I said, 'but there must be some reason why he was in Chester Passage.'

'Well, it wasn't chasing skirt,' said Dorkes sullenly. 'Not the Colonel.'

'What about the garage?' I said. 'Was it open this morning?'

'It was locked. The car had gone, but the garage was locked. That's what made me think the Colonel might have taken it into his head to go and visit you, sir. He'd been talking a lot about you, lately. He seemed worried.'

'I shouldn't think he was worried about me,' I said.

I had had more than enough of Dorkes. I wanted to get rid of him, but I wasn't sure how to do it without offending him.

'I don't know what your plans are,' I said, 'but there's really no point in you staying on here. There's nothing either of us can do. We shall just have to leave it to the Police, and hope for the best.'

'I ought to go and see the Old Lady,' said Dorkes. 'She'll be in a right state when she hears about this.'

'Your mother?' I said. 'Yes, I think you ought to do that.'

'The Colonel was always very good to her,' said Dorkes. 'She thought the world of him . . . we both did.'

'Where is she now?' I asked.

'She's in an old folks' place near Brentwood,' he said. 'Private, like. Her health's not good, and her mind's going. Well, she's getting on, and she's had a

hard life, Mr Charles. First my dad
. . . but that was war, wasn't it? I reckon
she could understand that, in a way. But
how am I going to explain this? Well, you
can't explain it, can you? Not sheer
bloody evil like this.'

'I'm sorry,' I said. 'Is there anything I
can do?'

'Well . . . ', he hesitated, and he
glanced warily over his shoulder. 'The
Colonel was paying for her at
Brentwood. I don't quite know what
I'm going to do now. She's happy there,
and a move would finish her. Of
course, the Colonel did say he'd look
after her in his will.'

'I expect he has,' I said. 'Don't worry;
I'll carry on with whatever arrangements
my father made until things get sorted
out.'

I regretted my generosity as soon as the
words were out of my mouth. A private
home? God knew what I had let myself in
for.

'That's very good of you, Mr Charles,'
said Dorkes. 'Very good indeed. It's a
great weight off my mind.'

I got out my wallet and found a five pound note.

'Please get your mother some flowers or something,' I said. 'Anything you think she'd fancy.'

'Oh, no, Mr Charles,' he recoiled. 'There's no need.'

'Please,' I said. 'I'm sure my father would have wished it.'

'Well . . . ' He took the money reluctantly. 'It's very good of you, sir. She's very fond of flowers. Always was.'

'I'll probably stay here, for the night at any rate,' I said. 'Leave me the keys. Where can I get in touch with you? There'll have to be an inquest and I expect we'll both have to attend.'

I thought for a moment he was going to argue, and then, reluctantly, he took a bunch of keys from his pocket, held between the residual three fingers and thumb of his left hand. Where the little finger had been was a wrinkled white stump. I tried not to see it.

'My address and number are in the Colonel's book,' he said. 'The address book in the desk.'

'Are you all right for money?' I said. 'I don't know what my father . . . '

His face darkened. 'I didn't do it for money,' he said.

'I know . . . ' I said quickly. 'I know that, Mr Dorkes. I just thought . . . You'll let me know if you need anything . . . or your mother.'

'You've got it all wrong if you think I did it for money,' he insisted. 'He looked after the Old Lady, and he stood by me when I was in trouble. I'd have done anything for him. A real gentleman, that's what he was . . . '

'I understand,' I said. 'I understand . . . and I'm very grateful for the marvellous way you looked after him . . . '

It was embarrassing. He faced me on the sofa, his large, clever, incomplete hands clenched together, his face muscles twitching, his brown eyes fixed upon me accusingly.

'No one knew . . . ' he started. Then he took out a spotless handkerchief and blew his nose violently. 'Even you didn't know, did you Mr Charles?'

'Know what?' I said.

He got up suddenly. 'Can I get you some more coffee, sir?' he said.

I shook my head. 'I think I'll go out and get some lunch. How about coming with me?'

He was collecting the cups together. 'No thank you, sir,' he said. 'Very good of you to ask me, but I couldn't stomach it. I'll just clear up, and then I'll go, if that's all right with you, sir.'

'Of course . . . ' I said, feeling thoroughly despicable. 'I hope your mother . . . I'll be in touch.' I hesitated, and then held out my hand. 'Thanks for everything, Edwin,' I said.

It was the first time I'd ever used his Christian name, and I regretted it as soon as it was out of my mouth. It sounded patronising, and worse, it sounded toadying. His expression told me what it sounded like, and how deeply he despised me. I stood, my hand held out idiotically while he carefully put down the tray he was carrying. He took my hand respectfully, warily and gently, as though it were a woman's and he was afraid he might damage it. But there was enough pressure there to let me know the crushing strength he was restraining.

'Thank you, Mr Charles,' he said.

7

The sleet had turned to snow, miserable, London snow, which seemed to collect the grime as it fell and to spread a disgusting grey mucus over everything. In Vernon Square I was lucky to find a taxi which had just delivered an exotic black girl outside one of the diplomatic missions. She was wearing a white fur coat and a colourful woollen hat. The inside of the taxi reeked of expensive perfume.

I drove to King Street, bought an evening paper, and dived into the first doorway which appeared to offer food. It called itself a Trattoria. It had Italian travel posters on the walls, and dusty plastic vine leaves trailing from the ceiling. It was after two, the lunch-time rush was over, and there was that stale, greasy, acrid smell that pervades restaurants with inadequate ventilation. But the lasagna wasn't bad, and while I ate I searched the paper for the 'Car Bomb' latest which the posters had promised. It told me nothing I didn't know already, and disguised lack of hard information with the dramatic experiences of Mr Ronald Carter (41) who was nearly thrown out of bed by the blast, and Mrs Bessie Maddox (57), an office cleaner who had been walking to work along Museum Street when the bomb went off. 'The whole pavement seemed to rise up at me,' she said. 'It was like the blitz.' The fire brigade had been on the scene a few minutes after receiving the first of hundreds of 999 calls, but they were too late to do anything but prevent the fire spreading to nearby buildings. 'There were a number of cars in adjacent lock-up garages,' said Chief Fire Officer Albert Perkins. 'If those had gone up, we should have had a major disaster situation on our hands.'

'Scotland Yard,' I read, 'have neither denied nor confirmed the report carried earlier on the BBC News that the car belonged to Colonel Vivian Rowlands, the sixty-three year old war hero and friend of

Marshall Tito. Although a call to the Irish Times claimed responsibility for the IRA, police are investigating the possibility that this was a hoax. This is the fourth car bomb incident to hit central London this year, and the authorities warn the public to take particular care, especially if they leave their cars out in the street all night.'

Which led me to wonder once again what on earth had induced my father to be parking in Chester Passage at that God-forsaken hour. He could, I suppose, have been visiting a prostitute. It seemed unlikely, but you never knew. Of course, if he hadn't been sleeping, as Dorkes said, he might conceivably have decided to get up and go for a drive round the empty streets; but if he hadn't left the car, how could whoever it was plant an elaborate bomb and several gallons of petrol inside without his knowledge. None of it made sense.

I didn't want to get back to the flat until Dorkes was out of the way, so I ordered coffee which I didn't want. It was luke warm and quite undrinkable. I smoked two cigarettes. Sitting in that hot, steamy atmosphere, the intense weariness that I had been fighting since five o'clock, overcame me. The effort of keeping my eyes open no longer seemed worthwhile. I knew that I mustn't give way, but I was too tired to move. My head sagged on to my chest.

'We're closing. It's three o'clock.'

I came to with a start, to find the young Italian cockney waitress purposefully clearing the table. With an immense effort I staggered to my feet, paid an extortionate bill and went out into the bleak November afternoon. The snow had eased, and I decided to walk back to Vernon Mews, in the hope that the exercise might wake me up.

It was half-past three when, cold, damp, my shoes sodden in slush, I let myself into the flat. To my relief, Dorkes had gone. There was something distinctly eerie about the still silence, the sense of utter desertion. There was no feeling that someone lived there, or had ever done so.

I forced myself to go through the rooms, starting with the bedroom, searching for some evidence that my father had existed here, or for a clue to his abrupt cessation.

The clothes, neatly hung in the wardrobe, seemed to belong to no one in particular, and the appearance of the neat, smooth bed denied that anyone had ever slept in it. It was the same in the bathroom where people usually leave their traces most obviously. The freshly laundered towels were untouched; the bath and lavatory bowl spotless; the soap new and the cabinet empty. In the kitchen, the fridge was empty, too, except for half a bottle of milk. There was no bread, either, nor any sign of food. This puzzled me and made me wonder what it was Dorkes had intended to serve my father for breakfast that morning.

In the living room, I went through the desk, but all I could find were impersonal business documents. The lease of the flat from the Westminster Settled Estates, Ltd., insurance policies, receipt for the rates; but no letters, no bank statements and no cheque book. The address book Dorkes had mentioned was there, bound in red leather. I glanced through it, and then put it in my pocket. I had a feeling it might prove to be important.

The flat seemed to be stripped of every vestige of a personality, of a human being, and I had the feeling that this had been deliberately contrived.

The bookcase contained mainly reference books, dictionaries, almanacks; no novels, but one biography — the English translation of 'Tito' by Milovan Djilas. I recognised this instantly as the one Tito had dedicated to the hero of Kjanek, but when I opened it, I was disconcerted to find that the flyleaf was missing — not torn out, but carefully cut, with a razor blade, I imagined. I was horrified; it was as though vandals had smashed some priceless work of art, or a church had been desecrated. It also seemed final and ineluctable proof of my father's extinction. I realised that the bomb was only the culmination of the process. Someone — was it my father himself? — had systematically obliterated the past. That someone had not been satisfied with his death; they had wanted, it seemed, to cancel out and expunge his entire life.

89

The weird emptiness played on my already over-taut nerves. It frightened me. I knew I could never stay there alone. I could never bring myself to sleep in that immaculate bed. I went into the hall where a white telephone was fixed to the wall. The directories were on a shelf below it, and I searched the yellow pages for nearby hotels. On my third attempt I booked a room at one called the Wellington, near Victoria Station. Then I remembered Frances, and I dialled the Duck End number. There was no reply. I tried again, just in case. No one answered. I wondered if she were still in bed.

The Wellington had obviously seen better days. Everything about it was slightly tatty and nothing was particularly clean. It catered for transients, travellers on their way to somewhere else, the cabin staffs of minor airlines, foreign tourists on a strict budget, and furtive couples who preferred to remain anonymous. My room on the second floor, however, was spacious and comfortable, and there was a private bath adjoining.

The bath itself, a massive, cast-iron monstrosity with claw feet, had black areas where the enamel had worn away, and yellowy stains of unknown origin. I didn't mind; it reminded me of the bath at Duck End, and any bath just then was something to sink into with gratitude, and not carp about. I was aching with fatigue; I felt shivery, dirty and thoroughly miserable. The water was hot and gushed out of the enormous tap in noisy spasms. I let it run at full throttle while I undressed, and then with grunts of bliss lowered myself into the scalding liquid.

I tried to put my mind into neutral and not to think about my father or bombs, or any of the unpleasant complexities which had suddenly disarranged my peaceful life. I lay back, closed my eyes and imagined drowsily that Frances was sharing the bath with me. My body responded to this mental eroticism with a half-hearted erection which I was too tired either to encourage or maintain. But even half an erection was better than nothing at that moment. At least it made some sort of sense, which nothing else had done that day.

I felt guilty about Frances. I had hurt her feelings, and I regretted now that I hadn't let her come with me as she had wanted. I didn't quite understand why I had rejected her, or why it had seemed so important to be alone.

I had never really recovered from the confusion of waking up on a morning in June two years before, in a strange room, and finding a tall, slim, dark-haired girl standing naked by the bed. She was posing, one hand on her pink hip.

'Anyone for hockey?' she'd said.

I was still struggling with the problem of where I was, when she climbed on to the bed and straddled over me. 'Wake up, Charlie,' she said. 'It's your birthday.'

She was damp and steamy and smelt of soap. Her breasts swayed gently over my face. It wasn't my birthday, but I didn't argue.

'Just what I've always wanted,' I said weakly.

I didn't like to ask who the hell she was.

Looking back, it seemed a curious

coincidence that this bizarre awakening came about because another man, of about my father's age, had been found dead in a car.

I had spent a week in Rome, in an effort to speed up the settlement of my mother's estate. On the morning I was due to fly back to Luton from Ciampino Airport, the body of Italy's one-time Prime Minister, Aldo Moro, was discovered in the boot of a car parked in the centre of the city. Moro had been abducted in broad daylight months before, and now the police looked extremely foolish and inept. They reacted with a spectacular show of slamming the door after the horse had bolted. War might have broken out, or a full-scale revolution. Ciampino, usually a sleepy, happy-go-lucky sort of place, reverted to its war-time role as a military aerodrome, as troops and police re-inforcements were flown into Rome. Civilian flights were completely disrupted and my charter plane, due to leave at two, didn't get airborne until nearly nine o'clock, and then made an unscheduled stop at Milan.

The long, nerve-racking wait, and the sense that we were refugees escaping, at the last minute, from a beleaguered city, broke down barriers of reserve and drew the passengers together for mutual support and protection. Because we seemed to be the only loners amongst a horde of package tourists, I struck up an acquaintance with a rather scruffy looking girl wearing jeans and a shapeless sweater, and loaded with plastic bags. I say 'girl', but actually she was only a year or two younger than myself.

On the journey we consumed the best part of a bottle of duty-free VAT 69. Later we both fell asleep, and when at midnight we touched down at Luton, she was sprawled across me, snoring gently, her black hair all over her face.

Normally at that hour the airport would have been closed, and various weary officials hurried us through the controls as fast as possible so that they could make out their overtime claims and get to bed.

'Well, goodbye, then,' said the girl. 'Thanks for the whisky.'

'Have you far to go?' I said.

'Ipswich,' she said.

'That's extraordinary,' I said. 'I'm going Suffolk way, too. Not far from Ipswich as it happens.'

'Amazing,' she said.

'Have you got transport?' I said.

'What's transport?'

'You won't get to Ipswich to-night,' I said. 'I've got my car here. I could give you a lift, if you like.'

'Thanks,' she said, 'but it wouldn't help. I'd just as soon hang about here until the trains start running. I expect I can find a chair or something to kip down in.'

'You don't want to do that,' I said.

'I haven't got much bloody option,' she said.

'There's a motel,' I said, 'not far from St Albans. We could probably get in there for the night and travel in the morning.'

'Is it free?' she said. 'All I've got is a return half to Ipswich and a pound note and two hundred lira.'

'You can owe me,' I said.

It had been an exhausting day, and

after all the whisky, I wasn't thinking straight.

'I'll go and find my car,' I said.

The morose, bleary-eyed night porter at the motel said they had only one room, and that was a double. The girl said she was too tired to care, so I signed the book as Mr & Mrs Rowlands. The room was dingy and the furniture looked as though it had been knocked down cheap at some second-rate auction. But at least it had a shower.

'Shades of 'Psycho',' she said.

She threw down her plastic bags and collapsed on to the bed. It creaked ominously.

'Any of that booze left?' she said.

I collected two grimy mugs from the shower cubicle and poured what was left of the Vat 69 into them. I sat down on the edge of the bed. It creaked again.

'What's your name?' I said.

'Frances,' she said. 'Frances Fairchild, would you believe?'

'I'm Charles Rowlands.'

She raised her mug in salute. 'Hi!' she said. 'Nice to know you, Charlie.'

'Are you a student?' I asked.

'Give over!' she laughed. 'I'm bloody nearly 30.'

'I'm not very good at ages,' I said.

'I'm an actress,' she said. 'I went to Rome because my agent said there was a film casting. It turned out to be one of these sex epics. They said I was too old and too skinny, anyway. How about you, with your Morgan and your natty gent's suiting. What are you?'

'I'm an artist,' I said. 'Well, a sort of artist. I do children's books, actually.'

'What age children?'

'Oh, any age before they start getting interested in sex and violence,' I said.

'Isn't that a bit boring?'

'It's about my level,' I said.

'Aren't you interested in sex and violence, Charlie?'

'I don't mind watching a bit of hockey,' I said.

She let her mug drop on to the floor and stretched herself out full length. She yawned. 'I'm married, if you're interested,' she said.

'Oh,' I said. 'I see.'

'Don't worry about it,' she said. 'The bugger pissed off a year ago. The last time I heard he was in Rhodesia.'

'My wife pissed off, too,' I said. 'The last time I heard she was in Rickmansworth.'

'Small world,' she said. 'God, I'm tired.'

I finished my whisky, staggered into the cubicle and splashed some water over my face. When I came back, she was under the covers, apparently dead to the world, her clothes scattered about the floor. I undressed down to my pants and eased myself gingerly into the bed beside her. I kept to the edge, careful not to touch her. Almost immediately, the combined effect of fatigue and alcohol overcame me. My last thought before I lost consciousness was that, one way and another, I was probably behaving very foolishly.

I had planned, on my return from Rome, to go and see my father. I frequently planned to go and see my father, but somehow, something nearly always cropped up at the last minute to make the visit inpracticable. I had become an expert in lulling my conscience with a variety of ingenious pretexts, and it was nearly six months since I had seen him.

It wasn't that I didn't get on with him, exactly. It was just that he had become a stranger with whom I had nothing in common. After five minutes, polite enquiries about health and comments on the weather exhausted, conversation came to a dead halt.

That morning I put it to my conscience as persuasively as I could. Was it my fault that Moro had been murdered? Could I possibly have forseen that I would get involved with a thirty year old actress whose husband was in Rhodesia, and whose version of hockey had almost wrecked the job lot motel bed? Wouldn't it be better all round if I put off my visit until a more convenient time?

We had breakfast at the motel, and it was nearly eleven before we got away and headed for Cambridge. I hadn't convinced my conscience, and the further east we got from London, the more guilty I felt. Instead of taking the by-pass, I drove into Cambridge and parked in Trinity Lane.

'I'm worried about my father,' I said. 'I'd better give him a call. I shan't be five minutes.'

I left Frances wandering round the market stalls while I found a kiosk. Dorkes answered the 'phone.

'Is Colonel Rowlands there?' I said.

'Who is that calling, please?'

'His son,' I said. 'Charles.'

'Oh, Mr Charles! The Colonel was only speaking about you this morning, sir. He was saying it was a long time since he'd seen you.'

'Is he there, Mr Dorkes?' I said coldly.

'I'll see, Mr Charles,' he said. 'I'll see if I can locate him.'

He always spoke as though the tiny flat were a fifty room mansion. I heard muffled noises in the background, and then my father's voice came on the line. It was a clipped slightly nasal voice, with just a trace of his native Yorkshire.

'Is that you, Charles?' he said.

'Hello, father. Yes, it's me. How are you?'

'Well enough,' he said. 'How are you?'

'Fine,' I said. 'I'm fine. I've just got back from Rome.'

'Oh yes?' he said.

'Listen, father,' I said. 'I intended to call in and see you, but things were pretty chaotic. This Moro business put everything out of gear. The flight was eight hours late and I didn't get in until after midnight.'

'Your mother knew Moro well,' he said.

'Yes,' I said. 'I believe she did. Dreadful business.'

'Never met him myself,' he said. 'But then I was never interested in politics, as you know.'

'Best to keep out of them now-a-days,' I said. 'Talking of Mother, by the way, I didn't achieve very much. Everything still seems snagged up in about twenty different ministries. God knows when things will be settled.'

'Are you short?' he said.

'No, no,' I said. 'I can survive. It's just so aggravating . . . '

'Come and see me if you're short,' he said.

101

'I'm coming, anyway,' I said. 'I've been meaning to for months, but what with one thing and another, I've been so fearfully busy. Deadlines to meet . . . '

'Dead what's?' he said.

'You know,' I said. 'Publication dates . . . deadlines.'

It was a lie, of course. My last Porker Family book had been published in May and I hadn't even started the next one.

'Oh,' said my father. He could never accept that drawing anthropomorphous pictures of pigs for the under fives was proper work for a grown man. There was a long, awkward pause. We seemed to have reached the inevitable, dreaded point at which communication ceased.

'Old car still going?' I asked, with a desperate brightness.

'Edwin's very good with it,' he said.

'They don't make them like that now,' I said. 'I reckon the old Rover will go on for ever.'

'But I shan't, old chap,' he said.

'Don't be morbid, father,' I said.

'Facing facts,' he said. 'You never know these days . . . look at Moro.'

102

There was another long pause.

'Well,' I said. 'I've no more change, so I'll have to go. I'll see you soon . . . next week, perhaps. Look after yourself.'

'Edwin looks after me,' he said.

'That's splendid,' I said. 'When I come I'll probably stay a night or two.'

'Don't leave it too long,' he said.

The call hadn't appeased my conscience; in fact, I felt guiltier than ever when I emerged from the kiosk into the bright June sunshine. I thought I had lost Frances, but I found her at last, surrounded by undergraduates and shifty looking men clustered round a stall which sold old records and well-thumbed girlie magazines. I had to drag her away from a copy of Penthouse.

'It pays well,' she said. 'Did you know they spray your pubic hair with lacquer?'

'No,' I said. 'I didn't know that. How about a drink?'

'You look as though you need it,' she said.

We both had gin and tonics in a pub that was all oak beams, horse brasses and duelling pistols. It was packed with foreign tourists.

'How's your father?' she asked when we had elbowed our way into a comparatively quiet corner.

'Strange,' I said.

'Is he ill?' she said.

'Not physically. Just strange. He's always been strange. Since the war, at any rate. He had a pretty rough time.'

'You mean he's mental?'

'I wouldn't say he was exactly normal,' I said.

'Was he shot down or something?'

'Thrown out, not shot down. He was parachuted into Yugoslavia. Fought with the Resistance.'

'Like that film,' she said. 'Secret something. Robert Taylor, wasn't it? Or Leslie Howard? Who was the girl?'

'Come on,' I said. 'I don't want a bloody parking ticket on top of everything else.'

I shut up about my father. I realised that to Frances the whole thing must seem as remote as Waterloo or even Agincourt. If it hadn't been my own father involved, I should have felt the same; and it *was* like an old film if you hadn't, like me, seen the real life sequel.

Frances had her own problems, as I discovered as we continued our journey. She was sharing a flat with a girl who worked in the Ipswich Rep. The theatre was due to close, and her friend had got a touring job in South Africa. Now the Italian film part she had been banking on had fallen through.

'I can't decide whether to go on the game or on the dole,' she said. 'What do you advise?'

'Why not come down to Duck End,' I said.

'What's Duck End, for God's sake?'

'It's where I live.'

'Sounds like it. Alone?'

'There're two cats,' I said. 'I shouldn't think they'd mind.'

She was silent for some time. Then I felt her hand resting lightly on my thigh.

'I'll have to collect my things,' she said.

I had that disconcerting impression that I was once again behaving very foolishly as I took my left hand off the steering wheel and put it over hers.

When I had said 'come down to Duck End' I had meant for the weekend. That was eighteen months ago. She was still there. I didn't quite know how it had happened, or more worryingly, how it would end.

And it was August before I got round to visiting my father.

8

I must have drifted off to sleep, because I suddenly became aware that the water was getting cold, and soap had congealed on the surface as a greyish scum. I dragged my mind from the past and my body out of the bath, and forced both to face the disagreeable present. It would have been hard to decide which showed the greater reluctance. When I had dried myself with one of the Wellington's bath towels, which were about the size of a baby's nappy, I put on the clean pair of pants Frances had packed, and studied my face in the steamy mirror. I looked ghastly, and I needed a shave, but I decided to let it go. All I intended to do that evening was to snatch a meal and go to bed. And the Wellington wasn't the sort of hotel where they'd notice a little stubble.

I took one step out of the bathroom and then I froze. Sitting on the edge of the bed was an extremely well-dressed man of about my own age. He had fair, waved hair, and between his legs he held a furled umbrella.

'Hello, there!' he greeted me. His teeth were Hollywood standard. 'I've been waiting for ages; I thought you'd disappeared down the plughole.'

I felt vulnerable and ridiculous; frightened and angry all at the same time. It was pure Kafka. The man on the bed seemed to find it all rather amusing. He looked me up and down.

'Venus arising from the foam,' he said.

'Who the ~~fuck~~ are you!' I said. I hoped my voice would be dominating and aggressive; but it emerged as a thin, craven croak.

'Surely you remember me, Rowlands,' he said. 'Julian Reece. We were at Uplands together.'

Vaguely I did recall a boy called Reece; but more clearly I remembered disliking him.

'They pushed your file on to me when they discovered we were old school chums,' he said. 'That's how their twisted minds work, I'm afraid. So sorry about your father, by the way.'

'You've got a bloody nerve!' I said. 'Breaking into my room . . . '

'Breaking in, Rowlands?' he said. 'Nothing of the kind. The door was unlocked. As a matter of record, I knocked several times. You don't expect me to lurk about in the corridor, surely?'

'What do you want?' I said. 'Are you selling something?'

'We don't sell things at the Foreign Office,' he said. 'Well, only State secrets, and only to the Russians.'

'You're from the Foreign Office?'

'More or less,' he said. 'An offshoot thereof.'

'How did you know I was here?'

'We have our methods.'

'The 'phone was bugged!' I cried. 'Is that it? The 'phone was bugged.'

'Don't get above yourself, Rowlands,' he said severely. 'You've no idea how important you have to be nowadays to get bugged. It's the latest status symbol. We're thinking of charging a fee.'

'How, then?' I said. 'No one knew I was coming here.'

'Quite simple, really,' said Reece. 'Legwork. A little man followed you. Of course, he did get a trifle wet. Operational hazard, I'm afraid.'

'Why in God's name should anyone bother to follow me?' I said. 'I still don't know why you're here, or what you want.'

'I thought we might have a little chat,' he said. 'Have you dined, as the vulgarians say?'

'Look here Reed, or whatever your name is,' I said. 'I've had just about all I can take for one day. I don't understand what's going on and I'm too bloody tired to care. I don't intend to chat or dine or do anything with you or anybody else. I don't care if you were at Uplands; I care even less that you're from the Foreign Office or an offshoot thereof. I am going to bed and I am going to sleep. So would you kindly ~~fuck~~ off and leave me in peace.'

'I know just how it is,' he said sympathetically. 'You'll feel very much better after a decent meal and an old

110

mate's ear to pour your troubles into. Shall we go somewhere really super. How about l'Ecu de France? HMG will pay.'

'I've told you,' I said. 'I'm not going anywhere.'

He got up. I was surprised how tall he was. His elegant clothes and his camp manner could not disguise an intimidating muscularity beneath the effete surface.

'Then we'll eat here,' he said. 'If you insist. I'll wait for you in the bar. Don't be too long, will you? One doesn't like to be seen hanging about a place like this.'

The fight went out of me; I surrendered. Apart from anything else, I was curious to know exactly what it was he wanted to chat about.

'Give me ten minutes,' I said.

★ ★ ★

I took twenty minutes, defiantly spinning out the time. When I went down, he wasn't at the bar; he was at the bottom of the stairs waiting for me in the dimly lit foyer.

'Ten minutes?' he said, reproachfully. He eyed me appraisingly, and it was clear he considered the time had been wasted. 'I've arranged for a nice quiet table, and checked for hidden electronic devices.'

'I'm going to have a drink first,' I said.

'All taken care of,' he said. 'Waiting for you at the table. Scotch.'

'Suppose I don't want Scotch.'

'Don't be difficult,' he said. 'I seem to remember you always were an argumentative bugger at school.'

The restaurant was even dimmer than the foyer. Either the management were trying to save electricity or they didn't want the customers to see what they were eating. The table Reece had arranged was against the wall in a corner. I noticed that the two adjacent tables had reserved cards on them, although no one arrived to claim them. An elderly, sad-looking waitress with bow legs and unconvincing terracotta hair took our order. Brown Windsor soup, steak pie, creamed potatoes and cabbage. Reece asked for the wine list.

'On the back, love,' said the waitress.

With an arthritic hand she grabbed the grubby, plastic covered menu he was holding and twisted it round.

'Care to choose?' he said.

'Leave it to you,' I said. 'I know nothing about wine.'

For some time he pored over the selection. 'I wish I didn't,' he said at last.

In the end he ordered a bottle of something called Entre Deux Rives.

'One number six.' The waitress whipped the menu away and hobbled off.

I took a gulp of the whisky which as he had promised was waiting on the table. 'Right,' I said. 'You wanted to chat: start chatting.'

He grinned at me with a dazzling dental display. 'You're the chap who does those Porker Family books, aren't you?' he said.

'What of it?'

'My niece Daphne thinks they're deplorable,' he said. 'I rather like them myself. Quite fun.'

'And how old is your niece Daphne?' I said.

'Six months,' he said.

We finished our whiskies in silence. Then he leant forward, his face arranged into an expression of intense sincerity.

'I really am terribly sorry about your father, Rowlands,' he said. 'Quite ghastly. I believe I met him once, one sports day.'

'Very unlikely,' I said. 'I don't think he ever came to a sports day. Not much point, really; I was such a complete duffer.'

He smiled reminiscently in an irritating way. 'Yes, you were, weren't you?' he said.

The Brown Windsor arrived. It looked like dark oak varnish, but it was hot and tasted quite good in a macabre way. Reece took one wary sip and then pushed his plate away.

'I'm going to be utterly frank with you, Rowlands,' he said. 'Cards on the table.'

'I wish you would,' I said. 'I shan't be able to keep awake very much longer.'

'An interesting character,' said Reece. 'Your father, I mean. I hadn't seen the files until yesterday. I found them quite absorbing.'

'What files?' I said.

'Just files,' he said. 'We keep files on all fellow travellers. That's our job.'

The loaded spoon on its way to my mouth stayed poised in mid air. 'Fellow whats?' I said.

'Travellers. People working for or with the Commies.'

For the first time that day I laughed. Soup slopped out of the spoon and splashed on the table cloth. Reece glanced around him, acutely embarrassed.

'It's not really amusing,' he said.

'It's hilarious,' I said. 'My father a spy! I've never heard anything so ridiculous in my life.'

'I didn't say spy.'

'Isn't that what you meant?'

'Not at all. We've no evidence of espionage.'

'Of course you haven't,' I said. 'The old man was the archetypal Tory. He thought the Daily Telegraph was a left wing rag.'

The waitress appeared with the steak pie and the Entre Deux Rives. She showed signs of wanting to go through the pantomime of tasting and approval.

Reece waved her aside impatiently. 'Just put it down,' he said. 'I'm sure it will be splendid.'

'Makes no odds to me, love,' she said, huffily. She plonked down the bottle and left us. Reece poured the wine.

'He fought for the Commies in the war,' he said.

'Wrong,' I said. 'He fought against the Germans. Besides, he hadn't much choice. It was a question of survival.'

'And he did survive,' said Reece. He tasted the wine, grimaced, and held the glass up to what little light there was. He eyed it incredulously. 'Mix this with the soup,' he said, 'and you could start a plastics factory.'

'If you can call it survival,' I said. 'I often thought he wished they'd left him to die at Kjanek.'

'Kjanek?' he said.

'Wasn't it in your files?' I said. 'The Kjanek massacre?'

'I believe it was,' said Reece. 'Something to do with caves?'

'That's where it happened,' I said. 'The Partisan unit my father was with and

116

hundreds of civilian refugees were holed up in the Kjanek mountains. The Germans had them surrounded and bottled up, but they couldn't get to them because only the local people knew where the caves were, and even if they had known, they wouldn't have been able to find them without a guide who knew the secret paths. The Montenegrins had used these caves for centuries to hide from invaders. There was only one snag; although they could just about exist by eating berries and tree bark, and the odd bird or animal they could trap, there wasn't any water. Water had to be fetched from a river in the valley, and that meant a dangerous climb at night into an area where the Germans were constantly on patrol. There were women and young children, and a lot of old people, and they knew they couldn't stay in the caves indefinitely.

'After about a month things were getting pretty desperate, so the main force went to reconnoitre an escape route through the German ring. My father and a young Yugoslav soldier were left to defend the caves. At night, they took it in turns to fetch the water in a couple of goatskins. One night, when it was the other man's turn, he didn't come back. They thought the Germans had got him; but it was the other way round. He'd got the Germans. He led them to the hideout at dawn the following morning. They were very thorough; first they used machine guns, and then, just to make sure, they threw grenades into the caves. My father was the only one left alive, and that was a sheer miracle.'

'I remember now,' said Reece. 'It was in the files. Actually, the way I read it, there were two survivors.'

'Two?' I said. 'Who was the other?'

'Why,' he said, 'the villain. The traitor. The man who went for the water.'

'God knows what happened to him,' I said. 'I always assumed the Germans killed him along with the rest.'

'Apparently they didn't,' said Reece. 'I suppose he'd done a deal with them, and they kept their side of the bargain. They let him go.'

'He wasn't there when the Partisans

came back and found my father buried under the bodies,' I said.

'Well, he wouldn't have hung about under the circumstances, would he?' said Reece.

'Anyway,' I said. 'What does it matter now? It's all ancient history.'

'I agree,' said Reece. 'It wasn't even much of a massacre, as massacres go.'

'There were others a lot worse,' I said.

'You'd have thought after all these years the Yugo's would let bygones by bygones. Put up some sort of commemorative plaque, and leave it at that.'

'There is a memorial,' I said.

'There's also Colonel Lenisec,' he said.

'Who is he?' I said.

'What he is now,' said Reece, 'is one of the Yugo's top intelligence men. What he was then was a common soldier in Tito's lot. His young wife and baby son were two of the victims of the massacre. He's not likely to forgive and forget. They're like that, you know — obsessed with revenge. He's spent his life hunting down the man who betrayed them.'

'The poor bastard's probably been

dead for years,' I said.

Reece shrugged. 'One thing's for sure,' he said. 'He will be when Lenisec catches up with him. According to the files there's a possibility he's in England, and the last thing we want is any more Balkan bodies lying about, stabbed with poisoned umbrellas, or whatever. We have a theory that, after the massacre, this chap escaped into Hungary, and then got into this country as a refugee when the Russians invaded in '56. A lot of odd characters got in then; we didn't ask too many questions.'

On top of the whisky, and combined with my fatigue, the wine was fast going to my head. I felt giddy and extremely confused.

'That's pure speculation,' I said. 'And, anyway, I don't see what it's got to do with my father.'

'He was working for Lenisec's organisation,' said Reece. 'Kjanek isn't the only score to be settled. There are quite a number of war criminals and traitors still on their list. They're like the Israelis, only rather more ruthless. They don't worry about decadent things like trials, for instance. The way they look at it is that they don't go after anyone who isn't guilty — or, put another way, — the fact that they're after somebody is sufficient proof of guilt.'

'You're wrong about my father,' I said. 'All he wanted to do was to forget.'

'You mean you never suspected?' said Reece.

'There was nothing to suspect,' I said.

'What about that Import-Export business he worked for?' said Reece.

'What about it?' I said.

'That was the cover they used.'

It was a shock. That Import-Export business had been mysterious. I had thought so in a vague way at the time, but I had never bothered much about it.

'Good God!' I said. 'If you knew all this, why didn't you do something about it?'

'He'd moved to Italy before we got on to it. Anyway, it didn't really concern us. He wasn't spying; no reason for us to interfere. But we kept a friendly eye on him, just to make sure he didn't get into trouble.'

'No,' I said. 'No. I can't believe it. You've got it all wrong.'

'But he did get into trouble, didn't he?' said Reece. 'Rather bad trouble.'

'You mean . . . there's a connection . . . with the bomb in the car?'

'We don't know,' said Reece. 'We'd like to find out, and we thought, or my boss did, that you could help us.'

'Sorry to disappoint your boss,' I said. 'I know nothing whatever about it. I knew he worked for some Import-Export Agency, but I never even knew where it was.'

I finished my glass and refilled it. I rather liked Entre Deux Rives, although of course, I wasn't accustomed to evenings at l'Ecu de France at the taxpayer's expense. Reece gave me an anxious glance; then he reached into his jacket and brought out a largish brown envelope.

'I think you ought to have a look at these,' he said.

Inside the envelope were a number of 8

× 4 photographs. They were obviously enlargements of negatives that hadn't been very good in the first place. But despite their fuzziness and lack of definition, I could recognise my father. In all the photographs, either with my father or close by, was another man of roughly the same age, stocky and chunky featured.

'Well?' Reece prompted.

'I can just about recognise my father,' I said.

'Nothing else?'

I studied the pictures again, concentrating hard to try and arrest the way they swam out of focus.

'I might be able to guess where some of them were taken,' I said. 'This one looks like Rome.'

'Good!' Reece looked pleased.

'And this one . . . Venice?'

'Splendid!' He was becoming almost jovial. 'This is rather like one of those deplorable quiz games, isn't it? That one you've got now, though. Rather more difficult.'

The photograph showed my father and

the stocky man on what appeared to be a seafront. In the background there were cliffs and white buildings which were probably hotels. My whoozy mind dredged up remote memories of family holidays.

'Bournemouth,' I said.

'Oh, dear,' he seemed disappointed. 'You drop points there, I'm afraid. Try a little further South.'

'The Med,' I said. 'Nice or somewhere.'

He clicked his tongue.

'Wrong ocean altogether. I suppose I shall have to tell you. That's Dubrovnik.'

'Why not?' I said. 'He often went to Yugoslavia. He had a lot of friends there.'

'Enemies, too?' said Reece.

'Why enemies? He was a National Hero.'

'You don't become a hero without making enemies,' said Reece. 'One of life's harsh facts, I'm afraid. I remember when I won the Victor Ludorum at Uplands, I've never been hated so implacably by so many before or since.'

'Not quite the same thing,' I said. 'You were quite insufferable. In my opinion,

Reece, someone in your offshoot has a very powerful imagination.'

'And someone had a very powerful bomb,' he said.

For a moment this jolted me into some semblance of sobriety. I was on the point of confiding to Reece the instinctive feeling that had been haunting me all day that my father's murder was linked with the Yugoslav struggle, and to tell him about the depersonalised flat and the missing page from Tito's biography. Before I could speak, the waitress returned.

'Want a sweet, love?' she enquired.

Reece hurriedly covered the photographs which I had put down on the table with his napkin.

'Just coffee for me,' he said.

'Yes,' I said. 'Just coffee.'

She collected the plates and dishes and departed with an indignant disapproving glare.

'She thinks you're peddling dirty pictures,' I said. 'Shall we finish the wine?'

'Entirely up to you,' he said. 'Don't involve me.'

He watched with an expression of distaste as I emptied the bottle into my glass. The urge to confide had passed. I didn't trust Reece. It seemed a very long time ago since I trusted anybody.

'There's nothing I can tell you,' I said. 'Somehow my father and I were never very close. He never talked about himself, or the war. All I remember is that, when I was about seven, he gave me his medals to play with.'

'Even his DSO?' said Reece.

'I don't know what they were,' I said. I wished I could stop talking quite so much, but the words kept spewing out as the dregs of the wine took effect. 'I know I swapped one with a boy at school for a Dinky toy — a fire engine, I think it was — and the next day the boy's father brought it to the Headmaster. There was a frightful row. They seemed to think I'd pinched the bloody thing.'

'A Dinky toy?' Reece mused. 'Not a bad swop as things have turned out.'

Once again we were interrupted by the waitress bringing the coffee. I offered Reece a cigarette, but he refused in favour of one of his own long, thin cigars.

'Have another look at those pictures,' he said. 'Have you seen the other man before?'

'Never,' I said. 'Who is he?'

'Milhailo Lenisec,' said Reece. 'I think you ought to know he's in London right at this minute. Under another name, of course. We'd rather like to know what he's up to.

9

Before Reece had walked uninvited into my bedroom, I had been bewildered; when he left me that night I was in a state of utter and complete confusion. I didn't know what to believe — not that it mattered. My beliefs could have no possible significance, except, perhaps, to myself.

I told myself that whatever my father may have done or been, it was nothing to do with me, and yet I couldn't shake off the unpleasant feeling or involvement, of being dragged against my will into the thick of someone else's nightmare.

I was frightened, too. I felt menaced, and I sensed that Reece had either been threatening me or warning me, especially since he had suddenly changed his tone, put on a show of false reassurance, and admitted that it was probably all nonsense and not to worry. Then he remembered he had to rush off somewhere, and was in such a hurry he forgot his promise that HMG would pay for our meal.

Before I staggered up to my room, I used the phone box in the lobby and tried the Duck End number again. There was still no reply. The plangent sound of the ringing tone filled me with ominous forebodings. I was convinced that Frances had packed her bags and left me, and I pictured two starving cats roaming a desolate house. I thought of calling the Doynes, but decided this would probably only lead to further complications.

There comes a point at which anxiety reaches the limit the human mind can bear, and a merciful defence mechanism comes into operation. That's what it seemed like, anyway. I could, of course, have reached another stage of intoxication. Whatever the cause, on my way up to my room, something went click; the burden lifted and I felt as though I were floating on a cloud of irresponsibility. 'Fuck all to do with me,' I said aloud. 'Let them get on with it.' What did I care if my father had been a spy, or Frances had decamped or the cats were starving. I

129

threw my clothes on the floor and crawled into bed. 'Fuck them all,' I said before I lost consciousness.

It was ten o'clock before I woke up. The long sleep had done me good, and although I had a minor hangover, the lie-back-and-enjoy mood had survived. Even the discovery, when I paid my bill, that the Entre Deux Rives had cost £4.50 did not depress me unduly.

It was too late for breakfast at the Wellington, but I found a café near Victoria Station where breakfast in the form of bacon, sausage, egg and tomato apparently went on all day.

While I ate, and drank two cups of rank tea, I read the Daily Express someone had left on the table. The Bloomsbury Bomb was no longer front page news. It had been pushed out by the arrest of a pop star for rape, the murder of a teenage girl in Coventry, and the latest appalling unemployment statistics. Tucked away inside was a short paragraph headed 'Tito's Friend Bomb Victim?' 'Chief Inspector Claydon,' I read, 'head of Scotland Yard's Anti-Terrorist Squad, who is in charge of investigations into Wednesday's car bomb outrage in Bloomsbury, said yesterday that he was not in a position to confirm or deny reports that the man killed was Colonel Vivian Rowlands, hero of the wartime Yugoslav Resistance and friend of Marshal Tito. It is understood, however, that the police are satisfied from evidence already in their possession that Colonel Rowlands, who has been missing since early Wednesday morning, was the victim. Home Office forensic experts are examining sacks of charred wreckage removed from the scene. The date of the inquest has not yet been fixed and will probably not take place until the results of the scientific tests are available.'

The bit about sacks of charred wreckage did not sit too easily on the bacon, sausage and egg, and I was glad to escape from the greasy fog of the café and into the open air. A bitter wind was whipping along Victoria Street carrying swirling flurries of snow. I walked briskly to the station and made a call to Granville and Burnett of Chancery Lane, who had been my father's solicitors, and who, with me, were his joint executors. At least, as far as I knew, I was one of the executors; as far as I knew, too, I was the principal beneficiary. Of course, he might well have changed his mind and made another will cutting me out. I couldn't blame him if he had, after the way I had neglected him, but it seemed sensible to find out.

Mr Granville's secretary said he would see me at twelve. Then I tried the Duck End number again, but there was still no reply. I decided that rather than involve the Doynes, I would try again after I had seen the solicitors, and if there was still no answer, make a dash back to Suffolk to find out for myself what was going on.

I took a taxi to Temple Bar, and since I had half-an-hour to spare, I had coffee in Twinings, opposite the Law Courts, where, in the privacy of high-backed booths, lawyers whisper to their clients, and Fleet Street journalists while away the time before El Vino's opens for business, working out their expense accounts on the margins of the early editions.

As I was leaving, I noticed a man standing at the counter where they sold packets of tea and coffee and boxes of chocolates. He was short, swarthy and wore a blue, belted raincoat and a black trilby hat. I had the feeling that I had seen him before, but I couldn't for the life of me think where.

While I was paying my bill at the cash desk near the door, the man passed me and went out into the street. When I followed, he had vanished.

As I crossed the road and walked up Chancery Lane, I was still cudgelling my brains, trying to remember who the man was; but it was not until I was climbing the dark, narrow stairs to Granville and Burnett's office, that the solution suddenly came to me. The man in Twinings was the chunky featured individual who had been in all the photographs Reece had shown me. I stopped dead on the first landing, outside a door marked 'Micklejohn & Sparks. Literary Agents.'

'Lenisec!' I said aloud. 'Bloody Milhailo Lenisec!'

A girl came out of the door, coat

draped over her shoulders like a cloak. She looked at me, startled, hesitated, and then said, 'Can I help you?'

I suppose she thought I was another eccentric author looking for Micklejohn or Sparks. 'No, no,' I said hurriedly. 'Thank you so much. I'm just on my way up to the next floor.'

'I see . . . ' She gave me a scared look and clattered off down the stairs.

I thought to myself, it can't be. There must be thousands of men vaguely resembling Lenisec, and, in any event, the photographs had been so indistinct I could hardly recognise my own father in them. I tried to dismiss it from my mind. All Reece's talk about 'fellow travellers' and 'mysterious organisations' had made me paranoic. The man was probably called Smythe, and had nipped into Twinings to buy a box of chocolates for his wife in Ealing. But I knew he was not called Smythe; I knew quite definitely that I had seen Milhailo Lenisec. And it could hardly be mere chance that he had happened to be in Twinings at the same moment as myself.

The couldn't-care-less euphoria had peaked and was now in rapid decline. I wished, oh God, how I wished, that I was safe and snug back at Duck End with my cats, my Porker Family, my electric blanket, and possibly Frances. I was no longer sure about Frances.

Adrian Granville was a small, rotund man with a bald head, several chins and enormous, owl-like spectacles. I had met him once when we had both been a good deal younger, just before my parents went off to Italy. He had been bald then, but I couldn't remember him having quite so many chins.

His room looked as though it had been assembled from a kit labelled 'Old-fashioned Lawyer's Sanctum'. The walls were lined with impressive books which were obviously never read, legal-looking documents tied with pink tape were littered about, and there was a massive silver inkstand on his desk. None of it seemed quite real.

In his wheezing voice he expressed his profound sympathy, and described his own intense grief and shock. None of this seemed real, either, and it was only when he started talking about the legal problems involved that he became credible. The main problem arose, I gathered, because no one would admit, officially, that my father was dead.

'It puts me in an exceedingly awkward position,' he said pettishly, as though my father, the bombers and the police had conspired, deliberately, to inconvenience him.

'What about the will?' I said. 'My father told me he had made me an executor.'

He looked shifty. 'I shouldn't really discuss that side of things,' he said. 'Until there is official notification of death, you really have no standing.'

'No standing?' I said. 'I don't follow you. I'm his son. I'm the next of kin. I've got to see to his affairs, pay his bills . . . arrange some sort of funeral, too, I suppose.'

'At this stage,' he said, 'you have no obligations whatever in the matter. As far as being an executor, legally an executor does not exist until death has been confirmed and the will proved. I realise that it is all very trying. These things can be trying.'

'They can indeed,' I said.

He hesitated, and then leant forward in his leather upholstered chair. He clasped his stubby hands together and became conspiratorial. 'I don't know to what extent your father confided in you . . . ' he said.

'Hardly at all,' I said. 'Actually we had rather lost touch.'

'Perhaps I shouldn't tell you,' he said, 'but the circumstances are unusual. During the past six months, Colonel Rowlands has been selling off his assets — rather unwisely, in view of the depressed state of the market. Mostly stocks and shares, but there was some property in Yorkshire. Of course, he may have been investing the proceeds elsewhere. He may have decided to buy paintings, or antiques. People do, you know. He didn't ask my advice. Frankly, I don't know how things stand at the moment, and, of course, I have no way of finding out until probate has been granted.'

'How peculiar,' I said. 'If he bought paintings or antiques there's certainly no sign of them at the flat.'

'Could have been gold or diamonds, or even stamps,' he said. 'On the other hand he may have needed cash for some purpose, although it would be a fairly substantial sum. It's only fair to tell you this, because the estate may be worth very much less than you might have thought. In fact, it may be worth practically nothing.'

'I'm afraid I don't understand it,' I said. 'Unless, of course, he was being blackmailed . . .'

'Nonsense!' he said sharply. 'I see no reason to jump to that extreme conclusion. No doubt there's a very ordinary explanation.'

'I've never had to cope with anything like this before,' I said. 'I'm told there will be an inquest.'

'I should think so, almost certainly,' he said.

'Is it necessary for me to be legally represented?' I said.

'Hardly necessary,' he said. 'But it

might be advisable.'

'I was wondering if you . . . '

'Of course,' he said. 'I'll get in touch with the Coroner's Office and find out what I can.' He smiled and fingered his chins. 'We can, perhaps, lend you a little moral support, if nothing else.'

'I could do with any amount of that,' I said.

★ ★ ★

Outside in Chancery Lane, the snow was coming down in earnest. It was lunchtime, and the pavements were crowded with the working population scurrying in search of food. I paused in the cover of the doorway and checked carefully to see if the man I had seen in Twinings was lurking anywhere nearby. He wasn't, as far as I could see, but all the same, I kept glancing nervously over my shoulder as I walked back towards Fleet Street. I got some nasty looks and one encouraging smile from a large woman whose feet were enclosed in plastic bags.

I made a suicidal dash across Fleet

Street and straight into the Cock Inn, which likes to encourage the belief that Johnson and Boswell were among its earlier patrons. The ground floor bar was packed, but upstairs, I knew, having once been treated by a publisher, was another quieter bar and a restaurant.

I sipped my gin, glanced idly through the menu, while the hum of muted conversation washed over me. I tried to compose myself, and to piece together the crazy jigsaw that was all jumbled up in my mind. But none of the bits fitted together, and I hadn't even got the box lid to see what the completed picture ought to be; but the feeling that the wild mountains of Montenegro would form the background was stronger now than it had ever been.

By the time I had eaten my roast beef and apple charlotte, and had lingered over my coffee, it was half-past two. There was a phone down in the cellar, next to the lavatory, and I tried the Duck End number again. There was no reply. I was relieved, in a way, because it enabled me to make a firm decision. I would go straight back to the flat, collect the

Morgan, and head for Suffolk.

The car was where I had left it, covered in a thin layer of snow. I threw my holdall in the back, and was about to get into the driving seat, when it occurred to me that my father might have come back and was up in the flat, alive and well and wondering what all the fuss was about. I knew it was a totally unrealistic hope, but I couldn't just drive off without checking.

I fumbled for the right key on the bunch Dorkes had given me, opened the front door and climbed the stairs. Immediately I entered the tiny hall, I knew something was wrong. I could smell cigarette smoke. It couldn't be my father because he never smoked cigarettes. It might, of course, be Dorkes who probably didn't smoke in the same way that he didn't drink; but he wouldn't have been able to get in because I had the keys. All I could think of was the man in the belted raincoat. Milhailo Lenisec. He was the sort of man who wouldn't need keys.

'Hello!' I called, absurdly, my voice quaking. 'Is anyone there?'

'Of course someone's here, you daft

bugger,' a voice replied from the living room. It was Frances. Relief flooded over me, but it was not to last long. No longer in fact than it took me to step into the room.

'Jesus Christ!' I cried.

The room which I had left so meticulously neat and orderly was now in a state of chaos. Frances was slumped in an easy chair amid the debris, hair over one eye, a cigarette dangling from her lips.

I surveyed, in horror, the raped mock Georgian desk, drawers gaping open, contents strewn over the green carpet; the books from the bookcase in a disorderly heap; the sofa stripped of its cushions which had been tossed across the room.

'God Almighty!' I was almost screaming. 'What is this? What the hell's going on!'

'The telephone's been repaired,' said Frances in a matter-of-fact tone. She jerked her head to encompass the shambles. A turd of ash fell from her cigarette. 'Apparently this is how the GPO engineers work up the smoke.'

'What engineers?'

'The engineers who were here when I rang the bell,' she added. 'Ten minutes ago.'

'How do you know they were engineers?' I demanded stupidly.

'They said so, didn't they,' she replied. ''Your telephone will be OK now, madam' they said. Then they shoved me out of the way and took off in a van. They left the door open, so I came in.'

I collapsed on the remaining easy chair. 'You saw them?'

'Of course I saw them. They bloody near knocked me over.'

'What were they like?'

'I don't know what they were *like*,' she said. 'I didn't have time to study them. Besides, I was somewhat taken aback.'

'Taken aback!' I exclaimed. 'Taken aback! The bastards have wrecked the place.'

'It's not too bad,' she said. 'I think I disturbed them.'

'Have you called the police?' I said.

'Actually,' said Frances, 'I thought they

probably were the police. Weren't they the police?'

'How the hell do I know who they were!' I buried my face in my hands. 'I don't know anything any more. The world's gone stark raving mad!' I looked up abruptly. 'What are you doing here, anyway, for Christ's sake?'

'I decided you needed me,' she said. 'It seems I was right.'

'But you were supposed to stay at Duck End!' I was on the verge of tears. 'Haven't I got enough on my plate?'

'I knew you'd be pleased to see me,' she said. With an effort she pulled in her legs and hoisted herself up. 'Did your old man keep any booze?'

'Only brandy,' I said. 'And that's all gone. In fact, every bloody thing's all gone, and if it wasn't before, your telephone engineers will have had it.'

'There must be something,' she said, getting up.

'Frances!' I pleaded. 'Will you listen? Listen . . . please! You're not supposed to be here. You're supposed to be at Duck End. That was the arrangement.'

'Your arrangement,' she said. 'Not mine.'

'You said you'd stay and look after the cats.'

'Sod the cats,' she said heartlessly.

'You can't just walk out and leave cats like that,' I said.

'Mrs Doyne,' she said. 'I gave her two quid and left fifteen tins of Super Pussy-din with added vitamins. Let them catch their own bloody mice if they're not satisfied.'

'They'll be cold,' I said.

'They've got fur coats,' she said. 'Which is more than I have.'

'I told you,' I said in desperation. 'I told you, Frances. I can't cope with you as well as all this . . . '

'Oh, shut up!' she said. 'Get on with your *crise de nerfs* while I find something alcoholic — if it's only hair tonic.'

She went into the kitchen, while I paced about the littered carpet muttering 'Oh, my God!' and 'Bastards!'

'It's OK in here,' Frances shouted. 'They haven't touched the kitchen.'

'I'm going to call the police,' I shouted back.

145

'You do that,' she said.

I went into the hall and dialled 999.

'I want to report a break in,' I said, when I got through.

'Break in?' The voice sounded disapproving, not to say suspicious. 'I see, sir. What is the name and address?'

I told him, and added a garbled version of what Frances had told me.

'Telephone engineers?' he said.

'That's what they said. The place is a shambles.'

'Vandals?' he suggested.

'You could say that.'

'Leave things as they are, sir,' he said. 'Don't touch anything. An officer will be round to see you.'

When I went back into the living room, Frances was framed in the kitchen doorway, triumphantly displaying a bottle.

'Johnny Walker,' she said. 'Under the sink, with the Fairy Liquid, the Jay cloths and the Kills all Known Germs Dead.'

'That'll be Dorkes,' I said.

'What will be Dorkes?'

'Forget it. How much is there left?'

'About half.'

'Well, don't stand there,' I said. 'Get the glasses.'

When she had poured the drinks, she raised her glass, smiled crookedly, and said in an unconvincing American accent: 'Here's looking at you, kid.'

I resented the way she was pre-empting the Bogart rôle.

'Of all the flats in all the world,' I grated out of the side of my mouth, 'you had to walk into this one.'

'I just followed the crowd,' she said. She took a gulp of whisky and collapsed into the easy chair. 'What did the filth say?' she asked.

'Frances!' I winced. 'Don't!'

'The fuzz, then,' she said. 'The Old Bill.'

'An officer will be coming round,' I said primly.

'What happened at the Yard?'

'Scotland Yard, do you mean? Nothing much happened at all. There was no point in all the panic. I might just as well have stayed at home. I wish I had.'

'Didn't you . . . you know . . . see . . . ?'

'See the body? No. They say it's unidentifiable.'

'But in that film with Walter Mathau,' she said, 'when they set the car on fire and burnt the girl's body . . . They can tell by the teeth.'

'We know all about the teeth,' I said.

At that moment the door bell rang. I leapt up, feeling for some reason absurdly guilty. I hurriedly finished my drink and pushed the glass into Frances' hand.

'Hide the booze!' I whispered urgently. 'And for Christ's sake, don't try and be clever. I'll do the talking.'

The bell rang again, a long, impatient peal.

'What are you so scared about?' said Frances, as she gathered up the evidence and made for the kitchen. 'You're the innocent victim, aren't you?'

'That's what worries me,' I said.

When I opened the front door, I received yet another shock. I had expected a uniformed constable, or, at the most, a low-ranking CID man from the local station. When I saw Chief Superintendent Barker standing there, my astonishment and consternation must have been obvious.

'Mr Rowlands!' he said. 'Surprised to see me again so soon, I expect.'

'Well . . . ' I stammered. 'Well, yes . . . I thought . . . '

'Understandable,' he said, stepping into the hall.

'The local lads called me as soon as they got your message,' he said. 'We can't discount the possibility that this incident is linked in some way with . . . ' He stopped short as he caught his first sight of the disaster area. He clicked his tongue. 'Oh, dear,' he said. 'Oh, dear me.'

'It may not be as bad as it looks,' I said. 'I don't think there's much damage.'

'Any sign of forced entry?' he said.

'No,' I said. 'But they use credit cards nowadays, don't they?'

'Really?' he said. 'Is that so?'

'So I've read,' I said.

He looked slowly round the room. 'Have you discovered if anything is missing?' he asked.

'I don't even know what was here in the first place,' I said.

But there was something missing, which I had noticed straight away. There were now only three framed photographs on the top of the bureau. Marshal Tito's had disappeared. I didn't tell Barker this for reasons I didn't properly understand. Perhaps I wanted to avoid any further complications. I didn't tell him about the page which had been cut from Tito's biography, either. I had the irrational feeling that by keeping quiet I was in some way protecting my father.

'This must be very distressing,' said Barker, 'under the circumstances.'

'It's not only distressing,' I said, 'it's downright terrifying.'

He took off his expensive black overcoat, folded it carefully and placed it reverently over the back of a chair. The mauve silk lining glowed with smug opulence.

'First things first,' he said.

'Certainly,' I said.

'I understand the intruders were disturbed,' he said. 'By a visitor? Am I right? Now who was that?'

'Me,' said Frances, appearing from the

kitchen, whisky glass, recently replenished, in her hand. She swept aside the curtain of hair that obscured her left eye, and hooked it behind her ear. 'I am the vital witness.'

'Oh, Frances,' I said nervously. 'This is Chief Superintendent Barker.' I made frantic faces at her, imploring her to behave. 'Mrs Fairchild.' I completed the introduction.

'Mrs Fairchild . . . ' He gave her a formal bow, which was acknowledged with what I supposed she imagined was a stately inclination of the head. Her hair came adrift from its moorings and fell across her left eye again.

'Do please sit down,' I said.

He lowered himself into the chair Frances had left.

'Will you have a drink, Chief Superintendent?' she asked.

Greatly to my surprise, steeped as I was in the lore of fictional policemen who always piously refuse to consume intoxicating beverages whilst on duty, he said: 'Thank you, Mrs Fairchild.'

'There's only Scotch,' she said. 'They

did leave us half a bottle. It was under the sink with the Fairy Liquid, would you believe?'

'Very kind of you,' he said. 'With a little water, if I may.'

'Oh . . . ' she said. 'Right . . . ' She disappeared back into the kitchen. I was gratified to note that his acceptance had taken some of the wind out of her sails.

'Mrs Fairchild is a friend?' he suggested.

'Yes,' I said. 'That is correct. A friend.'

'A friend of your father's?'

'No, of mine.'

'Ah,' he said. 'Does she live in the neighbourhood?'

'No,' I said. 'At the moment she lives in Suffolk — like me. A little village called Duck End.'

'Suffolk?' he said. 'Delightful countryside. Unspoilt.'

'Actually,' I said, 'she's an actress. You may have seen her on TV.'

'Commercials,' said Frances, entering again with a tray on which were arranged the diminished bottle of whisky, three glasses and a jug of water. 'Actually,

Charles and I live together. In sin, as they used to say.'

'As a young man,' said Barker, 'I had a hankering to go on the stage.'

Frances poured the drinks; I noticed with misgiving that her glass was empty again. She held up the bottle.

'Sweetie,' she said, 'we'll need fresh supplies, unless you fancy going on to the detergent.'

She sat on the arm of my chair in a pose of deliberate intimacy. I edged away as far as I could.

'Perhaps we can sort out the basics,' said Barker. 'You disturbed these intruders, it seems, Mrs Fairchild. How many were there?'

'Two,' said Frances. 'Well, two came out when I rang the front door bell, anyway.'

'Can you describe them?'

'Only vaguely. They didn't hang about. One was younger than the other. The old one had a sort of blue raincoat and the young one was wearing what you'd call a donkey jacket, I suppose. He was carrying some kind of leather bag. Then there was this van they drove off in; I think it was a Mini.'

'Colour?'

'Green, I think.'

'Did you note the number?'

Frances shook her head. 'I thought at that point that they *were* telephone engineers,' she said.

I had a disturbing sensation of *déja vu*, as Barker produced an envelope from his pocket, just as Reece had done the night before, and took out a pack of photographs.

'Do any of these ring a bell?' he said, handing them to Frances.

She removed her hair from her eyes and went through them, rather as though they were holiday snaps. He watched her face, intently.

'This one gives out a faint tinkle,' she said at last.

'May I see?' I asked, as she passed the photographs back.

It was a head and shoulders shot; the expression frozen, eyes glaring and startled. It was Milhailo Lenisec, as I had known intuitively that it would be. I tried hard to control the way my hand shook as I gave the photographs to Barker.

'You recognise him, too?' he said.

'No . . . ' I shook my head and gulped. 'Who is it?'

'You don't want to see the others?' he said, ignoring my question.

'No point,' I said. 'I didn't see the men.'

'You didn't, did you,' said Barker. He turned back to Frances. 'Is this the man who spoke to you?'

'I think so . . . I can't be sure.'

'Can you describe the voice?'

'You're sitting on my cigarettes!' she burst out accusingly.

Barker jumped up as though she had said he was sitting on a snake. 'I do apologise,' he said. He searched the cushions, feeling down the sides of the chair. 'They don't seem to be here.'

'Someone's got my bloody cigarettes!' declared Frances, aggressively.

'I expect they're in the kitchen,' I said. 'Don't make a fuss.'

'Oh, no!' she cried. 'No fuss, please! Nothing to make a fuss about, is there?

Only some poor old man blown to blazes in the middle of London. He was only your bloody father, for God's sake!'

'I'm afraid I don't smoke, myself,' said Barker.

Frances clapped her hand to her mouth as though she were going to be sick, and then rushed off into the kitchen. The door slammed behind her.

'Terribly sorry,' I said. 'She's very . . . All this has rather upset her.'

'Understandable,' said Barker. He stood over me, fixing me with a hard glare. 'I shouldn't like to think that you're not being open with me, Mr Rowlands.'

'Open?' I said. 'In what way am I not being open?'

'I think you did recognise the man in that photograph,' he said.

'You're not being quite open with me, either.'

'Oh?' he said. 'I'm sorry to hear you say that.'

'Why are you pretending not to know what happened last night?' I said.

'I am not pretending anything, Mr Rowlands,' he said, severely.

'But you know that Reece came to see me. You know who Reece is . . . '

'An old school friend of yours, I believe,' he said.

'That's not what I mean. Why didn't you tell me the Secret Service was involved?'

'Hardly the Secret Service,' he said.

'Well, whatever it is. If my father is suspected of working for the Yugoslavs, why didn't you tell me? Why am I being kept in the dark?'

'There is no intention of keeping you in the dark,' he said. 'This is a complicated case, and a number of lines of enquiry are being pursued, that's all. We have our job; other branches of the Security Services have theirs. As far as the police are concerned, at this moment in time, we are investigating the murder of an unidentified man. We have yet to establish that the victim was Colonel Rowlands. That is our first priority. Naturally, if some other agency has information which bears on the matter, we would expect them to pass it on to us. I am relying on you, Mr Rowlands, to do the same.'

'If I knew anything,' I said, 'I'd tell you.'

'But you did recognise the man in the photograph?'

'He looked something like the man in some photographs Reece showed me,' I said. 'That's all. I was told his name was Lenisec, and he runs some sort of organisation hunting down war criminals.'

'And you've never seen him, apart from in those photographs?'

'I don't know,' I said. 'I thought I glimpsed him this morning in Twinings, the coffee place opposite the Law Courts. I can't be sure . . . It was just an impression. I only saw him for a second.'

'If you see him again . . . or think you see him,' said Barker, 'or if you are approached, please let me know at once. Let me know . . . not your friend Reece. If I'm not in, ask for C11, extension 40. Someone will take a message. I've a couple of my chaps outside. If you don't mind, I'll send them up to have a look round. Test for fingerprints — the usual routine.'

I helped him on with his overcoat. It

was a materpiece of tailoring, and I eased it over his shoulders with the wary solicitude of a Christie's porter holding up a Ming vase.

'Do apologise to Mrs Fairchild for me,' he said.

'She'll be all right,' I said. 'She's . . . highly strung.'

'I could see that,' he said. 'Is there a husband, may I ask?'

'Is there a what?'

'A Mr Fairchild?' he said.

'There may be,' I said. 'In Rhodesia.'

'Ah, yes,' he said. 'A troubled country.'

I went with him into the hall. He grasped my hand and held it a fraction longer than seemed strictly necessary. 'You'll be staying in Town?' he asked.

'Not if I don't have to,' I said. 'I've got my work . . .'

'Of course,' he said. 'Thank you for your help. If there are any developments, I'll be in touch. Don't bother to come down. I can find my way.'

Back in the living room, Frances was re-installed in the easy chair. She held up Barker's glass. 'Didn't touch it,' she said.

'They don't,' I said. 'They never drink on duty.'

'He was weird,' she said. 'Did you see his coat? I thought only the Vice Squad could afford coats like that.'

'And the Special Branch,' I said.

The door bell rang again.

'Oh, Christ!' Frances swallowed Barker's neglected drink at a gulp. 'What now?'

'Two of the lads,' I said. 'Fingerprints — the usual routine. You'd better go back in the kitchen.

'I'm going out,' she said. 'I've got shopping to do.'

'Are you sure you're all right?' I eyed her anxiously.

'What do you mean 'all right'?' she demanded, belligerently. 'Why shouldn't I be all right?'

She did seem to have recovered her equilibrium quite remarkably. She was drunk, of course, but not noticeably more so than dozens of women who'd be doing last minute shopping in that part of London.

'Got enough money?' I said.

'If not, I'll Access it,' she said.

She went out as Barker's lads came in. One was an inspector and the other a sergeant. They were quick, efficient and silent, and were through in a quarter of an hour.

'Find anything?' I asked, as I let them out.

'Every little helps, sir,' said the inspector. I guessed, then, that he too, was probably Special Branch.

10

Frances was away so long, I began to get worried. She might have been run over, or run in for making an exhibition in a supermarket, or simply passed out on the pavement. I blamed myself for allowing her to go out, and I could imagine all sorts of unpleasant complications, as though there weren't enough already. Anxiety made me tense and irritable, and I thought why the hell couldn't the bloody girl have stayed out of the way in Suffolk. At the very least, she might have had the decency to stay sober.

I occupied the time clearing up the mess. When I had got things more or less back to normal, I sat down, chain smoked and tried to plan what I was going to do now that Frances had turned up — assuming, of course, that she wasn't in gaol or in hospital. The idea of sharing my father's immaculate bed with her appalled me, and I decided that it would have to be another night in a hotel. I didn't fancy the Wellington again, and I was in the hall searching the Yellow Pages for alternatives, when the front door bell rang.

It was Frances. She looked flushed and dishevelled, but otherwise unharmed. She was carrying a bulging plastic carrier bag. 'Have they gone?' she said.

'Of course they've gone,' I snapped. 'Hours ago. Where have you been?'

'Shopping,' she said. 'Where do you think?'

'It's bloody nearly seven,' I said. 'The shops don't keep open as late as this.'

'Some of them do,' she said.

She pushed past me; the plastic bag made chinking sounds as she moved.

'You've tidied up, then,' she said, looking round. 'Did the fuzz find any clues?'

'Every little helps?' I said. I followed her into the kitchen. 'Did you really recognise that photograph? Was it one of the men?'

'Didn't know him from Adam,' she laughed, theatrically. 'I just wanted to please the Super.'

'He wasn't pleased,' I said. 'He doesn't like hysterical females.'

'I wasn't hysterical,' she said. 'I was drunk. I still am, slightly.'

'You made a bloody exhibition of yourself,' I said. 'It was embarrassing.'

'So did you,' she said.

She began unloading the plastic bag, announcing each item as she placed it on the table. 'One whisky, one gin, three tonics. Eggs, butter, milk, cheese. So called French bread, two tins Boeuf Bourguignon, slightly damaged hence three p. off. Two strawberry mousse, mousses or mice. One packet spaghetti, just in case, tomato sauce . . .'

'I don't know why you bought this lot,' I interrupted. 'We're not staying here.'

'I've only just come,' she said. 'I'm not going back to-night.'

'We're going to a hotel,' I said.

'What's wrong with this place?' she said.

'Everything's wrong with it. It gives me the creeps. Besides, there's only one bed.'

'How many beds do you need?'

164

'It's my father's bed,' I said. 'Can't you see, it wouldn't . . . well it wouldn't be right. I already feel like a trespasser. Suppose he were to suddenly walk in . . .'

'Face facts, Charlie,' she said. 'You know damn well he won't walk in.'

'Well, I'm not going to dance on his grave,' I said.

'So now it's dancing,' she laughed.

'We're going to a hotel for to-night,' I said. 'Tomorrow we'll go back to Duck End. I'm opting out.'

'Running away, you mean,' she said.

'As fast and as far as I can,' I said.

'Well, we might as well eat first,' she said. 'Can't waste this lot. How about an omelette?'

'Christ, no!' I said. I knew what happened when Frances made omelettes; half the eggs landed on the floor and the finished product on the ceiling.

'The Boeuf Bourguignon, then?' she said. 'Go well with this.' She delved into her bag and brought out a familiar looking bottle.

'Special offer,' she said proudly. 'Only

165

one, thirty-nine.'

I looked at the label. It was Entre Deux Rives.

'OK?' she asked.

'Fine,' I said. 'Wonderful. Mix this with the Bourguignon and we can start a plastics factory.'

I left her to it. I couldn't bear to be a witness as she set about defiling the kitchen Dorkes had left so virginal. I went into the hall and was relieved to find that the door was equipped with two bolts. I felt slightly better when I had fastened these securely. Then I started ringing up hotels, but they all were full up, or said they were, and I was on the point of calling the Wellington again, when Frances shouted that grub was up.

I didn't know what state the kitchen was in, although I could guess; but she'd done a fair job with the Bourguignon. The pseudo French bread was a bit soggy, but at one, thirty-nine the Entre Deux Rives was a definite bargain, considering what the Wellington had charged for it. She'd switched on the television, and we sat on the sofa, our plates on our laps, and watched the last part of a venerable British film. It was a cops and robbers epic of appealing innocence. The cops all had posh RADA accents, and the crooks spoke an unconvincing Elstree Cockney which was positively Dickensian. We played our favourite game of anticipating the next line of dialogue, which wasn't taxing, and by the time the film came to its predictable end — a chase up a high structure — the bottle of Entre Deux Rives was empty and I was feeling almost glad that Frances was there. She rose even further in my estimation when she revealed that her shopping spree had included a botty of Rémy Martin.

'Special offer?' I asked.

'Access,' she said.

'Good old Access.'

I knew I ought to phone the Wellington before it got too late, but somehow the brandy seemed to take the edge off the urgency. A pleasant lethargy engulfed me and I couldn't even summons the energy to switch off the television. The screen was now filled with talking heads mouthing imcomprehensible jargon about the 'Balance of Payments Situation', and what effect it would have in the 'context of the short term', at the 'end of the day', and even 'across the board'. What it came down to was that things were in their usual mess situation, which I knew already.

'The bastard said my father was working for the Communists,' I said.

'Which bastard's this?' said Frances.

'The bastard called Reece,' I said. 'He barged into my bedroom at the Wellington last night. He said he was from the Foreign Office, or an offshoot thereof.'

'Was he?' said Frances.

'God knows,' I said. 'He was at school with me . . . one of these clever sods. Always winning things.'

'Not him,' said Frances. 'Your old man. Was he a spy?'

On the screen the quartet of heads was getting quite upset about the 'Gross National Product'.

'I didn't believe it at first,' I said. 'It seemed too utterly absurd. But now, I'm not so sure. There's something very peculiar going on.'

She got up and switched off the television. 'You'd better tell me,' she said. 'Perhaps I can help.'

'I don't see how you could help,' I said.

She came back to the sofa, lowered herself on to my lap and put her arms round my neck. 'I could look after you,' she said.

'You reckon?' I said.

Somehow it no longer seemed important to phone the Wellington. I still had my inhibitions, but they had weakened considerably. By the time I had helped Frances to pull her jersey over her head, and had undone her bra while she wriggled out of her skirt, they had given up the struggle and slunk away to sulk in the dark undergrowth of my mind. A bed, after all, was a bed. And why go traipsing across London to find one when there was one a few yards away in the next room.

The inhibitions, guilt and conscience emerged the following morning, fully armed and refreshed, and came looking for me with a vengeance. When they found me, in my murdered father's monastic bed, stark naked, with Frances stark naked beside me, they set about me unmercifully.

Frances slept on, blissfully unaware of my ordeal. She had that satisfied, slightly bruised look which in happier circumstances would have made me feel quite pleased with myself. Even then, as I endured my punishment, I experienced the onset of those symptoms for which, at Uplands, an immediate cold bath had been the recommended cure.

Before I got myself into even deeper trouble, I forced myself to get up. I staggered into the sitting room where I vaguely remembered having left my clothes. I drew the curtains, and, as the bleak light of a London November seeped in, what was revealed acted on my libido as efficiently as the iciest bath.

The havoc Milhailo Lenisec and his mate had wreaked seemed mild and amateurish in comparison with the chaos Frances had created, or, in any event, instigated. There was the messy debris of our supper, our abandoned clothes, including a pair of tights, limp and shrivelled, hanging over the television. The sofa looked as though it had served as the arena for an all in wrestling contest.

It was ten o'clock and I had a ghastly premonition that Dorkes was going to arrive at any moment. I retrieved sufficient clothes for decency, and then gathered up some of the greasy plates and went into the kitchen. How anyone could have contrived quite such a shambles heating up two tins of boeuf bourguignon defeated me. I desperately needed a cup of tea, so I put on the kettle, and then went back into the sitting room for a cigarette. I couldn't find them, and I was on my hands and knees searching under the sofa when I heard Frances saying, 'I wondered where you'd got to. What are you doing down there?'

'Playing woofwoofs,' I said tartly. 'What do you think?'

'If you're looking for cigarettes,' she said, 'there're some in my bag.'

'And where's your bag?'

'A good question,' she said. 'What's the time?'

'After ten,' I said. 'We'll have to get this place cleaned up before . . . ' I stopped short; the shock of her appearance robbed me of speech. She had my sheepskin coat draped over her shoulders. It hung open as though she were posing for the centre spread of a girlie magazine.

'For Christ's sake!' I said.

'What's wrong?' She looked innocent.

'Get dressed!' I said. 'Supposing someone comes in?'

'Who's going to come in?'

'Dorkes, for one,' I said.

'I don't know why you're so scared of Dorkes,' she said.

'I don't want to be on his list for castration,' I said.

'I'm going to have a bath,' she said. 'I feel sticky. By the way, did you know the kitchen was on fire?'

I wheeled round and saw clouds of white vapour billowing out of the half open door. I dashed into the kitchen which was obscured in a dense fog of steam from the boiling kettle. I switched it off and started waving a drying up cloth about.

'It's the kettle,' I shouted.

'You can bring me a cup of tea in the bath,' she shouted back.

It had been my plan to start back for Duck End right away; but Frances, when she had bathed, dressed and drunk two cups of tea, decided, since she was in London, she might as well have her hair done at a place in Sloane Street.

I didn't argue. In fact, I was rather glad to get her out of the way while I cleaned and tidied the flat; and if Dorkes or anyone else appeared, I preferred her not to be there.

There was a lot to do. I washed up, tidied the kitchen, hoovered the sitting room, plumped up the cushions, cleaned the bath and made the bed. Then I packed, and was about to take the bags down to the car ready for instant departure when Frances returned.

I was struck immediately by a change in her manner. She looked distracted and anxious, and she made none of the expected comments about my housewifery. She didn't even demand an appreciation of the Chelsea hairstyling. She ignored me, went straight to the window, and peered out intently.

'So you've had it cut,' I said. 'I think I like it.'

She didn't answer.

'I've packed all your stuff,' I said. 'Shall we get going? Frances! Can you hear me? What are you staring at?'

She turned slowly, her expression tense and solemn. 'I'm being followed,' she said.

'Don't talk bloody rubbish,' I said.

'Not so much followed as lurked,' she said.

'What does that mean?'

'There was a man lurking outside when I left here. When I came back he was still there. Now he's lurking in the courtyard.'

'Imagination,' I said. 'Chelsea's full of men whose principal occupation is lurking.'

'Have a look for yourself,' she said.

I joined her at the window. In the

courtyard, standing by the Morgan, was a stocky, elderly man wearing a long, black overcoat and an astrakhan hat. As I moved the net curtain aside to get a better view, he looked up. I stepped back hurriedly.

'Is that him?' I said.

'Of course it's him.'

'Have you seen him before?'

'Don't start doing a Barker. No, I haven't seen him before, and no, he's not one of the telephone engineers. What are you going to do about it?'

'Me?' I said. 'There's nothing much I can do. He didn't molest you, did he? I suppose I could call the police and say there's someone acting suspiciously, but that would only lead to more complications. He's probably perfectly innocent — not interested in you at all.'

'The courtyard's private property, isn't it?' said Frances. 'Go down and ask him what the hell he wants.'

'For all I know,' I said, 'he could have a perfect right to be there. He may be waiting for someone — he could even be a tenant.'

'Does he look like a tenant?' she demanded. 'Anyway, if he is, he can say so. Are you scared, or something?'

I moved cautiously back to the window. The man had begun pacing up and down, to keep warm, probably. He didn't look very formidable, but you never knew. Within the recesses of that voluminous overcoat, I visualised an armoury of guns and knives.

'Yes,' I said.

'What are you?' exclaimed Frances, contemptuously. 'Man or mouse?'

She didn't wait for an answer. She pushed me aside, a fierce light in her eyes, her jaw set with determination.

'Where are you going?' I quavered.

'I'm going to sort him out,' she said. 'I'm not scared, if you are.'

'Frances!' I pleaded. 'Be sensible. We don't want any more trouble . . . '

'Oh, shut up mouse,' she said. 'Get back in your hole.'

I hesitated whether to follow her, but decided, cravenly, that, strategically, it would be wiser to stay where I was and cover her from the window. I took up my position behind the net curtains and saw her appear in the courtyard. The lurker immediately started to make for the entrance, but she ran after him and stood in his path. He tried to edge round her, but she foiled him with quick footwork. Frances gesticulated; the lurker gesticulated. Then they both turned their heads and looked up at my window. She pointed; he shook his head and made another attempt to escape, but Frances took his arm and steered him firmly towards the front door. I heard their footsteps on the stairs, and, a moment later, Frances pushed the man into the room. If I was scared, I was relieved to see that he was clearly terrified.

'This is Mr Radowski,' she said.

'Oh,' I said.

'He has a hotel in Brixton,' she said.

'No . . . no . . . ' The man made deprecating gestures. 'No hotel.' He spoke with a thick, mid-European accent.

'What does he want?' I said.

'You'd better ask him,' said Frances.

'Please, sir.' Radowski became agitated. 'Please, sir. I beg your pardon. I think I must go. I should not have come here. I am not wantink to make no trouble.'

'Now you're here,' I said, 'you may as well tell me what it's all about.'

His eyes shifted from side to side, like a trapped animal. He seemed to be contemplating flight, but Frances barred the way.

'It is about the gentleman who was killed by that terrible bomb,' he said. 'Captain Rowlands.'

'Colonel, actually,' I said. 'He was my father.'

'I am sorry, sir,' he said. 'I think I have made a mistake. I will go now.'

'You'd better sit down,' said Frances. 'Take off your coat.'

'No!' He clutched the lapels of his coat protectively. But he did sit down, perching on the edge of the sofa.

'Would you like a drink?' I said.

'It is early for drinkink.' He shook his head.

'Coffee, then?' said Frances. 'You must be cold, hanging about outside all day.'

'Nothink!' he said. 'Nothink, please. Already I am being too much trouble.'

'Are you Yugoslav?' I said.

He gave a violent start, and gazed at me wild-eyed.

'Why you say that?' he demanded. 'Why you say Yugoslav?'

'No reason,' I said. 'I just thought . . . '

'I am Polish,' he said. 'Thirty years I have been in this country, but still I am Polish. I wish to be British, but there have been difficulties. Not of my own fault, you understand, but always there have been difficulties.'

'I'm sorry,' I said. 'You say you have come about the gentleman who was killed by the bomb. Did you know him?'

'No,' he said. 'Only the name I am knowink. I will tell you. The lady said I had a hotel, but that is not right. It is my bad English, I think. I have a house, a big house . . . many rooms. There is only Mrs Radowski and myself; the rooms we do not need we let to gentlemen. Gentlemen alone, you understand. No ladies . . . It is not suitable for ladies.'

'You have a big house and you take in lodgers,' I said. 'What has all this got to do with Colonel Rowlands?'

'Please, sir, I will explain,' he said. 'There is a gentleman livink in my house for a year now, we call him Mr Archie.'

'Mr Archie?' I said, convinced now that the man was mad.

'He has a strange name,' said Radowski, 'so we call him Mr Archie. He is Hungarian, I think . . . a refugee from the Russians. I am sorry for him because I was also a refugee. I know how bad it is for a refugee.'

'And what has Mr Archie got to do with me or my father?' I said.

'He is gone,' said Radowski.

I glanced enquiringly at Frances, who shrugged and shook her head.

'What do you mean 'gone'' I said.

'For three days now,' insisted Radowski. 'For three days he is gone. He has left everythink — all his clothes — everythink.'

'And he owes you money, I suppose?' put in Frances.

'No, no.' Radowski shook his head violently. 'He left plenty money. In his room there is a box full of money. Always he worked . . . in a hospital, I think, but I do not know which hospital. There are so many hospitals. He had no friends . . . no ladies. Perhaps sometimes he drink a little, but he is never no trouble. Some of the men in my house, they are not nice. They are dirty and lazy, but Mr Archie, he is always clean . . . always he is working. Never make no trouble. Mrs Radowski, she cook him good meals, she wash his clothes. I try to be a friend, I try to help, but . . . '

'Mr Radowski,' I interrupted his tirade. 'I don't know why you have come here. If you are worried about one of your lodgers, you should go to the police.'

'No, no! No police!' he said. 'I am not wantink no trouble with the police.'

I looked at my watch; if I didn't get rid of him soon I could see that we would be stuck there all day. I got up.

'I'm sorry,' I said. 'But there's nothing I can do about it . . . '

'He left with me a letter,' said Radowski.

'A letter?' I sat down again.

'The last time I see him, when he went out of the house, he gives me a letter.

'Please to keep this for me,' he say, 'and if they kill me, take it to the Yugoslav Embassy'. That is why I am surprised when you say Yugoslav. Why Yugoslav? Yugoslav is nothink to me. I am not wantink to take the letter. I say, no one is going to kill you, my friend. I thought he was a little . . . how do you say?' He tapped his forehead.

'Crazy,' supplied Frances.

'Yes, yes. I thought it was all crazy talk. Sometimes when he drink too much, he talk crazy. But now he is gone, I am worried. I do not know what I should do.'

'I still don't understand why you have come to me,' I said. 'Or what it has all got to do with my father.'

He looked shifty. 'I will be honest,' he said. 'I will be quite honest. What do I know about Mr Archie? All the time he is livink in my house, and I know nothing. So . . . so Mrs Radowski, she steams the letter open with a kettle. It is to protect ourselves, you understand.'

'I'd probably have done the same myself,' I said.

'There are many pages,' he said, 'but all the writink is in a language I do not understand. Mrs Radowski who come originally from the Ukraine, she can understand a little. Not much, she is not educated, you understand. She think it is about the war, and there is many times written Captain Rowlands, and in English there is this address.

'What did Mr Archie write about the war and Captain Rowlands?' I asked.

'I am tellink you,' he said. 'Mrs Radowski can understand only a few words. But now there has been this terrible bomb, and Mr Archie is gone, I am frightened. That is why I take the liberty to come here.'

'Where is this letter now?' I asked.

'Mrs Radowski lock it away,' he said. 'I say we should burn it, but she say, no. Can you help me, sir? Can you tell me what I should do. I am not wantink to make trouble.'

'Unless I see the letter, I don't know how I can advise you,' I said.

'I am wantink you should see the letter,' he said.

'Can you read Serbo-Croat or whatever?' asked Frances.

'I could make a copy and get it translated,' I said.

'Let's go, then,' she said. 'Where did you say you lived, Mr Radowski? Brixton?'

11

There wasn't room in the Morgan for Radowski, so we took a taxi. The Pole sat tensely on the occasional seating facing us. Despite the freezing weather, his putty coloured, pock-marked face gleamed with sweat, and his stubby hands quivered. His nervousness increased as we left the West End and penetrated further and further into a wasteland of seedy streets and decaying buildings. We were soon well beyond the limits of the normal taxi beat, and the driver seemed as lost and confused as I was myself. At last he found his way to Palmerston Terrace, a cul-de-sac of shabby houses with basements, and steps up to the front doors. Some of these doors had been painted in gharish primary colours, and, parked along the kerb, were battered Ford Zodiacs and Zephyrs, some half dismantled and others decorated with psychedelic designs. There were groups of West Indians, wearing woollen tops, lounging against the area railings, and, as soon as we stopped, a cluster of multi-coloured infants gathered to inspect us.

'Got your passport, mate?' the driver enquired as I paid him.

The children followed us up the steps of number 12, until Radowski rounded on them and told them to bugger off. They retreated, uttering shrill, disrespectful remarks in incongruous cockney voices.

Inside the dark, narrow hallway, the air was rancid with the smell of bodies and frying.

'Please,' said Radowski. 'You wait, please.'

He disappeared into the dark recesses beyond the staircase. Frances gripped my arm.

'I'm right behind you, Charlie,' she whispered nervously.

'There's plenty of room up front,' I whispered back.

Frances' grip on my arm tightened as the stairs creaked, and an unsavoury figure, obviously one of Radowski's gentlemen lodgers, in a ragged raincoat, filthy plimsoles and several days stubble, shuffled down. He sidled past us, wheezing, adding his own pungent reek to the foetid hall.

'Meths,' breathed Frances, as the front door closed behind him.

'That's the least of it,' I said.

'I feel slightly sick,' said Frances.

Radowski re-appeared, holding a large bunch of keys.

'Please to follow me,' he said.

He led the way up the stairs. The carpet ceased at the first landing. We went up two flights of bare boards, past closed doors behind which muffled sounds of coughing and transistors issued. When we reached the top of the house, he unlocked a door and we squeezed into a tiny attic room with a sloping ceiling. There was an iron bedstead, a chest of drawers and a wicker chair.

'This is Mr Archie's room,' said Radowski.

In contrast to the squalor of the rest of the house, this room was astonishingly neat and clean. The bed was carefully made and covered with a purple counterpane. In its seedy way it reminded me of my father's flat. It had the same aura of soldierly discipline and barren masculinity.

'He leave everythink,' said Radowski. 'Everythink. All his money . . . look, I show you.'

He bent down and pulled from under the bed a fibre suitcase. He snapped open the catches and raised the lid. It was stuffed with banknotes, and most of them seemed to be twenties.

'Look!' said Radowski. 'Too much money. It is bad, all this money. Why should he go away leavink all this money?'

'The letter,' I said. 'We came to see the letter.'

'I wanted first you should see the money,' he said, closing the case and pushing it back under the bed. 'Now you know I am tellink the truth. How much you think? One thousand? Two thousand?

'Quite a lot,' I said.

'All the time he is livink in my house,' complained Radowski, 'I am feelink sorry for him. I not charge him much rent. Mrs

188

Radowski, she is cookink his meals, washink his shirts. We think he is a poor man. Where is he gettink so much money?'

He led the way back down the stairs, continuing his resentful monologue. Back in the hall he took us along the dark passage and then down some steps into a basement kitchen. Here the smell of frying and garlic was overpowering. A large woman, her frizzled grey hair sticking out around the margins of a greasy head-scarf, was chopping lumps of bloody meat on the top of a littered wooden table. As we entered she held the cleaver raised, regarding us with a mixture of astonishment and apprehension.

'This is the lady and gentleman comink to see the letter, missus,' said Radowski.

She dropped the cleaver and uttered something between a scream and a gasp. She clasped her bloodied hands to her massive breast. 'You police!' she cried.

'It's OK, missus,' said Radowski impatiently. 'OK. You get the letter . . . '

She began to jabber at him, frantically,

in a language I assumed was Polish. He reacted violently, shouting and waving his arm. For some time they harangued each other incomprehensibly. Then he turned to me, his face aghast. 'She is sayink the police have been and taken the letter,' he said.

She nodded vigorously. 'Policeman come,' she confirmed. 'He say he want Mr Archie's letter. You also policeman?'

'No,' I said. 'No, I'm not a policeman. When was this?'

'An hour,' she said. 'Perhaps an hour . . . ' She turned on her husband. 'I tell him, wait for Mr Radowski, but he say, 'No, give me the letter or there will be trouble for you' . . . '

'You crazy, missus!' Radowski screamed. 'You crazy, woman?'

'What you wantink I do?' she screamed back. 'You wantink we go to prison? You wantink trouble?'

'Trouble!' Radowski slapped his forehead despairingly. 'Trouble! It's all bloody trouble. I wish to God I never seen that bloody letter. Now they will come askink questions. Pokink, pryink.

They will find the money. All my life it is the same think. Always questions, questions. Germans, Russians, Americans, British . . . all askink questions. When I come to this country I work in factory. Day and night I work; Mrs Radowski, she work, cleaning filthy trains . . . '

'Hard work!' Mrs Radowski nodded vigorously, 'Bloody dirty work . . . '

'I save money,' continued Radowski. 'For thirty years I am workink and savink. Now all I am askink is a little peace in my old age, but now it will start again, questions, questions . . . '

'You've no need to worry,' I said soothingly. 'You've done nothing wrong.'

'What can I do?' moaned Mrs Radowski. 'Can I say, 'bugger off?' You wantink I should say that?'

'This policeman,' I said. 'What was he like?'

'What like?' she shrugged. 'How do I know what like? All alike to me, bastards . . . '

'Was he in uniform?' I said. 'You know, helmet and all that?'

'No, no,' she shook her head decidedly.

'Big policeman. High up. Inspector, he say. All I am seeink is his hand.' She held up her own sausage-like left hand, the little finger curled into the palm. 'Like this, no finger here.'

'Are you sure?' I asked astounded.

'You think me blind woman?' she demanded angrily. 'You think me stupid? Not able to count?'

Seeing my obvious consternation, Radowski rounded upon me with fierce suspicion. 'You are knowink this policeman?' he asked, sharply.

'No,' I lied. 'No, I don't know him.'

I was conscious of Frances pinching my arm. 'We'd better go,' she said.

★　★　★

Outside in Palmerston Terrace, it had begun to rain, a relentless icy drizzle. It had been a grave mistake, I realised, to have let the taxi go. There wasn't a chance of finding another in that area, and the only thing to do was to start walking in hope of eventually hitting a main road. The woollen tops had taken shelter, but a few hardy kids were still playing around the beaten up cars. A determined posse followed us until we turned the corner.

'What was all that about, then?' said Frances.

'I don't know what it was about,' I said. 'But I do know Dorkes has the little finger of his left hand missing.'

'The ubiquitous Dorkes,' she said.

'Too ~~fucking~~ ubiquitous,' I said.

'What are you going to do?'

'Do? I'm going to do what I said. Go back to Duck End and stay there. I'm sick to death of it all. Let them get on with it. The poor old man's dead, and that's it as far as I'm concerned. Whatever mess he was mixed up in, I just don't want to know. I'm getting out before I'm dragged in any deeper.'

'Meanwhile I'm getting soaked to the skin,' said Frances. 'Can't we get a taxi?'

'Not a chance,' I said. 'Ever been on a bus?'

'Those red things?' she said.

Cold and sodden, we reached Brixton Road and tagged on to a disconsolate queue at a bus stop. We boarded the first red thing that appeared to be going vaguely in the right direction. We climbed up into the dank fug of the upper deck. It smelt something like Radowski's hallway, and sounded like a ward for chronic bronchitics. I wiped a peephole in the condensation that obscured the windows and tried to keep track on where we were going. Eventually I glimpsed the leaden river and realised we were crossing Westminster Bridge.

'This'll do,' I said.

The bus stopped in Whitehall, and as we got off I was astonished to see Reece sitting on the rear seat of the lower deck. I grabbed Frances' arm and dragged her off on to the pavement.

'Let's get out of here, quick!' I said.

It was hopeless, of course. He caught up with us on the corner of Parliament Square.

'What's a nice boy like you doing on a number 3?' he said. 'And Mrs Fairchild, isn't it? How delightful. I'm Julian Reece.'

'Or an offshoot thereof,' said Frances.

'Jolly good!' he laughed heartily.

'If you don't mind,' I edged away.

'We're in rather a hurry.'

'Then we'll take a cab,' he said. 'HMG will pay.'

'HMG already owes me eight pounds fifty,' I said.

With an imperious wave he brought a cruising taxi to the kerbside. 'Vernon Mews, isn't it?' he said. 'Is that Kensington or Knightsbridge?'

'Chelsea,' I said.

'Of course,' he said. 'Chelsea.'

I hesitated, but Frances was already climbing in. 'Come on,' she said. 'I'm bloody saturated.'

Like Radowski earlier that day, I found myself relegated to the uncomfortable occasional seat while Frances and Reece lounged in comfort.

'Reece,' I said. 'I'm sick of this. Why are you tailing me?'

'Still suffering from delusions of grandeur,' he grinned. 'I'm not particularly interested in you, old dear. But I am curious about your Polish friend who's been careless enough to lose a lodger. What did he want with you, by the way?'

195

'It will save a lot of trouble all round,' I said, 'if I tell you now that I'm opting out. I don't know what's going on, and nobody seems inclined to tell me, so I'm retiring while I still have some vestige of sanity. No need for any more of this cloak and dagger nonsense. If you want me in future the address is Duck End Farmhouse, Duck End, Suffolk.'

'That doesn't answer my question,' he said.

'I don't have to answer your questions,' I said. 'In fact, the police have more or less told me not to.'

'For Christ's sake!' Frances snapped. 'Tell him. What difference can it make?'

'I expect he already knows,' I said.

'Try me,' said Reece.

★　★　★

It was one o'clock by the time we got back to Vernon Mews. Reece did pay for the taxi, but only, I suspected, as a means of insinuating himself into the flat. Frances disappeared into the bedroom to change into some dry clothes, while Reece leant against the radiator and eyed me quizzically.

'So you're going back to your rural retreat?' he said.

'Yes,' I said, 'and don't try and stop me.'

'Wouldn't think of it,' he said. 'I don't blame you. London's pretty foul at this time of year.' He looked round. 'But this is a jolly nice little flat.'

'I loathe it,' I said.

'You know,' he said, 'I find your tale of the mysterious letter no one can read, and the *soi-disant* policeman with the missing finger frightfully intriguing. It has the authentic Sherlock Holmes flavour.'

'I always thought Holmes was a bore,' I said.

Frances came back. She had abandoned her skirt and had put on her old jeans and sweater. She had also retrieved from the holdall I had been at such pains to pack, the bottle of Remy Martin of which we had drunk only about half the previous evening.

'Keep out the damp,' she said.

'Excellent brandy,' said Reece, eyeing

her approvingly when she had fetched glasses and poured us all a dose. 'Excellent.'

'It hasn't been paid for yet,' I said sourly.

'All the better for that,' said Reece. He drained his glass and absent-mindedly filled it again from the bottle Frances had left on top of the bureau. 'Does anyone pay for anything now-a-days?' he asked rhetorically. 'The dear old Brothers at Uplands taught us we paid for our sins, but even that seems to have gone by the board. Do you pay for your sins, Mrs Fairchild?'

'She Accesses everything,' I said.

'Call me Frances, Julian,' she said, smiling at him in a flirtatious way I found objectionable.

'You know, Charles,' said Reece, sippng his third brandy, 'It might be amusing if we paid the digitless Dorkes a visit.'

'Oh, no!' I said. 'Oh, no!'

'Just a friendly chat,' he said.

'Have all the friendly chats you like, Julian,' I said, with a sarcastic emphasis on the name. 'Have all the friendly chats you like, but count me out.'

'No harm in finding out what he's up to,' said Frances. 'You're responsible for him, in a way.'

'I am not responsible for anyone!' I shouted.

'He knows you,' said Reece. 'You can say I'm an old friend or something. We don't want to alarm him.'

'How many times do I have to tell you?' I was verging on hysteria. 'I've washed my hands of the whole wretched business.'

'He lives in Fulham, doesn't he?' said Reece. 'Just down the road. Only take a few minutes.'

'I don't care where he lives,' I said. 'I refuse to be involved, and that's final!'

'We'll grab a cab,' said Reece. 'HMG will pay.'

'Oh, shut up, for Christ's sake!' I said.

★   ★   ★

Dorkes' address in my father's book was 14 Chandos Road. This turned out to be a decayed backstreet shop, with a Methodist chapel on one side and a derelict house, boarded up and liberally daubed with graffiti, on the other. Reece peered through the dirty window at the jumbled display of spare electrical parts and second-hand appliances. There was a closed sign hanging inside the door, which was firmly locked.

'Waste of time,' I said. 'Let's go.'

'Closed for lunch, do you think?' said Reece.

'You didn't expect to find him waiting for us here, did you?' I said.

'Not really,' he said. 'I wonder if there's a back way.'

Reluctantly I followed him down a narrow alleyway beside the chapel and through a gate into a small yard, littered with old fridges and washing machines. There was a motor-bike covered in a plastic sheet. Reece knocked on the back door, and, when there was no response, tried the handle. The door opened and we stepped into a kitchen which displayed the same military order as the kitchen at Vernon Mews before the arrival of Frances. Another door led into a dim passage and the staircase. Reece called:

'Hello! Anyone there!' He waited, listening to the reverberation of his own voice. 'No one here,' he said. 'You can always tell.'

'Let's get out of it, then,' I said. 'We're trespassing.'

'Visiting,' said Reece. 'The door was open.'

'Trespassing,' I said.

He ignored me and started to climb the stairs. I cursed the fatal weakness of character which had allowed me to be coerced into this absurd and potentially dangerous situation. But curiosity, and the thought that Reece was probably armed and afforded some protection, compelled me to follow.

There were two rooms leading off the landing. One was ajar, and Reece kicked it fully open with his foot. For some moments we both stood rooted to the threshold, immobilised by the scene of chaos that faced us.

'Someone got here before us,' said Reece.

'Telephone engineers,' I said.

'Very thorough, whoever they were,' said Reece.

Gradually, as my mind adjusted to the shambles, I worked out that the room was, or had been, a combination of office and workshop. There was a roll-top desk, and, on its side, a Captain's chair. Under the window was a work bench strewn with tools and apparatus, while the floor was littered with books and papers.

'Stay where you are,' Reece commanded sharply. 'Don't touch anything.'

He picked his way delicately through the debris, delving amongst it with his gloved hands.

'Holy Christ!' he breathed. 'I thought Dorkes was in the electrical business.'

'So he is,' I said. 'He mends washing machines and things. Clever with his hands.'

'Lucky to have any hands left,' said Reece. 'Do it yourself bomb making. It's all here — explosives, timers, fuses, remote control. Some of it's army stuff ... some of it's IRA. Where the hell did he get it all?'

'He was in the SAS,' I said.

'What he's in now is trouble,' said Reece. He picked up a green covered folder and leafed through it. 'Jesus!' he exclaimed. 'They don't even let them see this at Camberley.'

'That solves it then,' I said.

'My boss won't be at all pleased,' said Reece ignoring me. 'This whole affair is becoming a monumental fuck-up.'

'At least we know now it was Dorkes who murdered my father,' I said.

'Do we?'

'I should say it was obvious. Up until now its all been like a jumbled jigsaw puzzle; none of the pieces seemed to fit. It must have been Dorkes — he had the opportunity, he had the know-how, and he could have had any number of motives. I never trusted the bastard. The only mistake he made was to give an out-of-date codeword when he phoned the Irish Times and put the blame on the IRA.'

'I was never much of a hand at jigsaws,' said Reece.

'We'd better call Barker right away,' I said.

'All in good time,' he said. 'Have a look in the other room — but don't touch anything, especially if you find the body.'

'What body?' I said.

He shrugged. 'There's almost certain to be a body somewhere,' he said.

I went out on to the landing and into the adjoining room, putting on my glove before I turned the knob. I didn't want my finger prints plastered about the place. I peered in apprehensively, expecting to find another scene of chaos and possibly carnage, but everything seemed undisturbed and in perfect order. The room was furnished as a bed sitter with a divan, covered with a paisley pattern counterpane against one wall. There were carefully arranged scatter cushions and a chinzy armchair. It could have belonged to a fastidious whore.

'Ponce's paradise,' said Reece, joining me at the doorway.

'They don't seem to have touched anything here,' I said.

'Probably found what they wanted in the other room,' he said.

'No body, either,' I said.

'Then there's not much point in hanging about,' he said.

'What about the police,' I said.

'Better leave things to me,' he said. 'If I were you I should make yourself scarce.'

'I intend to,' I said. 'If it hadn't been for you I'd be half way to Duck End by now.'

Outside the rain had started again and Chandos Street was deserted. We walked to the Fulham Road and got a taxi.

'I can see it all now,' I said. 'If, as you say, my father was involved with the Yugoslav Intelligence, they'd naturally be upset when he was blown up like that. They'd want to make sure there was no evidence lying about to link him with them. That's why they turned over the flat. It looks now as though they're on to Dorkes . . .'

'Do you know,' Reece said, looking at his watch, 'I haven't had any lunch . . .'

'As for Radowski, I reckon he's an accomplice of Dorkes. All this story about the missing lodger and the letter is just a blind to confuse the issue.'

'It certainly does that,' said Reece. 'You know, Rowlands, I should stick to the Porker Family. The plots are simpler.'

He leant forward and tapped on the

glass partition. 'I'll drop you here, if you don't mind,' he said. 'I've got to get back to the office fast. By the way, you're not thinking of leaving the country, are you?'

'I told you,' I said. 'I'm going back to Suffolk.'

'So you are,' he said. 'Lucky man.'

As I was getting out, he caught my arm. 'Here's another bit to fit into your jigsaw,' he said. 'Radowski's lodger was the other man in the caves at Kjanek. The one who went for the water.'

Before I could answer, he pushed me out and slammed the door. The taxi drew away, leaving me standing on the pavement of Sloane Street in the pouring rain.

I got back to Vernon Mews, wet, cold, tired and hungry. But I was still determined to go home that afternoon. Frances had made some sandwiches, and while I ate them, she brewed up coffee, adding the remains of the brandy.

'You didn't find Dorkes, I suppose,' she said.

'No,' I said. 'And the telephone engineers had got there before us.'

'Much damage?' she said.

'Quite a mess,' I said.

'I didn't think you'd find Dorkes,' she said. 'As a matter of fact, he rang up just after you'd gone.'

'Dorkes did?'

'Well, I think it was Dorkes,' she said. 'He didn't actually give his name, he was in such a state.'

'What sort of state?'

'He sounded shit scared to me,' she said.

'What did he want?'

'He wanted you, but when I said you weren't here, he got really incoherent. Then there was a lot of banging and thumping and the phone was slammed down.'

'Exactly what did he say?'

'It didn't make much sense,' she said. 'Not to me, anyway. Something about goats.'

'Goats?'

'That's what it sounded like; I could be wrong. Mean anything to you?'

'Not a thing,' I said.

'Perhaps it's some sort of code,' she said.

'So now it's codes,' I said.

12

During our absence the cats had gone on strike against Pussydin. Turned their snouts up at it, according to Mrs Doyne, when I telephoned to tell her we were back. She'd been obliged, she said, to buy them liver. There'd been some heavy snow, and the roof of the barn had finally collapsed, as Dad had always said it was entitled to do.

What with snow and patches of black ice, it was half past seven by the time we got home. The first thing I did was to switch on the electric blanket. Then I lit the fire, while Frances fried up some bacon and eggs. After we had eaten we lounged in front of the television. Clive and Sarah, who clearly didn't intend to forgive and forget the way we had deserted them, until we had undergone a probationary period of exemplary behaviour, did relent sufficiently to take up their accustomed positions on the hearth rug. They groomed themselves in a martyred sort of way, occasionally giving us oriental glances of reproach.

The sound of the television merged into a meaningless jumble, my eyelids drooped and I drifted off to sleep. I woke up with a violent start when a cushion hit me in the face.

'You're snoring,' said Frances.

'Rubbish,' I said. 'I never snore. What's the time?'

'Ten o'clock,' she said.

'Christ, I was tired!' I said. 'I must have dropped off.'

'You made enough noise about it,' she said. 'You woke me up, snoring.'

The television was still going. In close up a girl was eating a bar of chocolate flake in an obscenely suggestive way. It was the last advertisement before the ten o'clock news. It was the same old stuff; an uproar in Parliament over public spending cuts, another strike at BL, another bomb in Belfast, and the body of a man, shot through the head, found in Epping Forest.

'Turn the bloody thing off,' I said. 'I

just can't take any more misery.'

'Wait a minute,' she said. 'There may be something about Dorkes.'

'What makes you think there'll be something about Dorkes?'

'He could have been arrested, or something,' she said.

'Well, I don't want to know,' I said.

There wasn't anything about Dorkes, so I switched the television off and wandered into the kitchen to fetch two glasses and the whisky.

'A quick slurp,' I said, 'and then bed. I hope I never live through another day like this one.'

'You know,' said Frances, as we drank our nightcap, 'I'm sure it was Dorkes who phoned. He was scared — really scared.'

'So am I,' I said. 'I'm terrified I'm going to be landed with his bloody mother.'

'What's his mother got to do with it?'

'I've inherited her,' I said. 'My old man paid for her in some private home. God knows what it costs.'

'Why?' said Frances. 'Was she his mistress?'

'Never occurred to me,' I said. 'I should think it highly unlikely.'

'Perhaps Edwin is his illegitimate son,' said Frances. 'You could be brothers.'

'Don't make things worse than they are,' I said. 'You know what Reece told me? He told me to stick to the Porker Family — the plots were simpler. Well, that's precisely what I'm going to do. I'm starting work tomorrow, and nothing's going to stop me. Not the Yugos, or the IRA, or the Police, or bloody offshoots of the Foreign Office.'

'What about Ma Dorkes?' she said.

'Sod Ma Dorkes,' I said. 'Let's go to bed.'

The electric blanket received me, enveloping me in its warm embrace like a mother a long lost child. I missed the weight of the cats on my feet, but as I dozed off, I felt the familiar burden descend. I turned over and put my arm around Frances.

'They've forgiven us,' I murmured.

All Frances did was groan.

When I woke up it was snowing, the flakes fluttering down past the dormer window like a plague of white moths. I was alone; Frances had gone and so had Clive and Sarah. The unreliable travelling clock stood at half-past nine, so it could have been quite early, or possibly very late.

I reached out a hand into the freezing air and turned the blanket switch up to full power, snuggled down into a glorious private fug and then tried to concentrate on the mental jigsaw which, yesterday, I thought I had completed, but had now disintegrated into a pile of incompatible pieces.

I arranged them this way and that, but the picture still eluded me. There were either too many pieces, or not enough, and where goats fitted in to it all I couldn't imagine. Somehow, though, I felt, instinctively, that this was the key piece around which all the others would fall into place.

I heard Frances coming up the stairs, and pretended to be asleep.

'Tea,' she said. 'I've a good mind to chuck it over you.'

I opened my eyes reluctantly, and I

could sense at once that I was not in favour. 'What have I done?' I asked innocently.

'Nothing,' she said. 'That's your trouble. I thought you were going to start work today.'

'It's snowing,' I said.

'That's no excuse for pigging it in bed all day.'

'It's only half-past nine,' I said.

'It's bloody near eleven.'

'I wish you wouldn't mess about with the clock,' I said. 'I'm completely disorientated.'

'That's nothing to do with the clock. Do you want this tea or not?'

'Get into bed with me while I have it,' I wheedled. 'I'm not a solitary drinker.'

'No way!' she said. 'You're going to work and someone's got to fight through the blizzard to get supplies, unless you want to starve. That means me, of course.'

'You sound just like a nagging wife,' I said.

She flushed. 'I've been thinking about that,' she said. 'We can't go on for ever like this.'

'Like what?'

'You know very well like what.'

'Are you contemplating bigamy?' I said. 'It's you who'd end up in Holloway, not me.'

'Oh, we know you're fireproof,' she said bitterly.

'I'm singed round the edges,' I said.

She was clearly in one of her moods. They were like sudden, unpredictable squalls at sea; you just had to batten down and ride them out.

While I sipped the tea, she sat down on the edge of the bed, in a determined 'let's have this out' sort of way.

'I dreamt about Frank last night,' she said.

'Frank who?'

'My husband, Frank. I dreamt he was shot in the bush.'

'That could be painful,' I said.

'The Rhodesian bush, idiot!' she said. 'It was so real. If I'm a widow, it makes a difference.'

'I can't see it makes much difference,' I said. 'Unless you get some sort of pension. That would come in handy, the way things are going.'

'You're so utterly self-centred,' she said.

I took her hand. 'That Sloane Ranger hairdo suits you,' I said. 'I never knew you had such sexy ears.'

She snatched her hands away and jumped up. 'You won't get round me that way,' she said, and flounced back down the stairs.

I crawled out of bed, took my dressing gown from its nail and followed her. I found her in the kitchen, smoking a cigarette and reading the Guardian. She ignored me while I made myself some toast and brewed up a fresh pot of tea. She continued to stay hidden behind the paper when I sat down opposite her with my back to the Aga. While I munched my toast I read the headlines. They seemed to be an almost exact repetition of the night before's television news.

'Do you have to make that horrible noise,' she said.

'I'm eating toast,' I said.

'Well, eat it quietly, for Christ's sake. Which finger did Dorkes have missing?'

The sudden change of subject confused

me. 'What are you on about now?'

'Dorkes. Which finger hadn't he got?'

'The little finger on his left hand. Why? What's that got to do with me eating toast?'

'Read this,' she said. She folded the paper and handed it across the table. 'Body in Forest.'

'Yesterday evening' I read, 'the body of a man shot through the head was found by a courting couple in Epping Forest, near the small Essex town of Pringbourne. The body was concealed in undergrowth a few yards from the road. The Essex Police, who have mounted a major murder investigation, have issued a description of the man as being in his thirties, medium height, with brown eyes, black, close-cropped hair and a guards type moustache. The little finger of the dead man's left hand is missing, and apparently had been amputated some years ago. An Eire passport in the name of Murphy was found on his person, but a Police spokesman said that there is reason to believe this is a forgery. It is thought

216

that the killing took place elsewhere and the body dumped in the forest. There have been several similar cases of bodies being found in Epping Forest; the most recent was in 1974 when . . . '

'Good God!' I said, putting the paper down. 'It must be Dorkes!'

'I told you he sounded scared to death,' she said.

'Poor old Dorkes,' I said. 'Reece said there'd be a body somewhere.'

'What are you going to do?' she said.

'I don't see why I should do anything. I don't want to get involved.'

'You keep saying that. But you are involved, whether you like it or not. If you keep quiet, it'll only cause more trouble in the end. They could get you for obstructing justice, or something.'

'It may not be Dorkes at all,' I said. 'We could be jumping to conclusions.'

'Then there's his mother,' she said.

'Oh, hell!' I covered my face with my hands. 'What a bloody mess. There seems no end to it.'

She came round the table and put her arm round my shoulders. 'I'm sorry,' she said. 'Honestly I'm sorry. I haven't been much help . . . '

'We've both been under a strain,' I said.

'You'd better call Barker,' she said.

'I don't know what to do,' I said. 'I'm not properly awake yet . . . '

And then the phone rang, and the decision was taken out of my hands. It was Barker calling me.

'We think there's been a development, Mr Rowlands,' he said.

'Yes,' I said. 'I was just going to call you. I suppose it's this body in Epping Forest.'

'I hoped you might be able to help,' he said.

'I've just read the description in the paper,' I said. 'It sounds as though it may be Mr Dorkes.'

'We would like you to be able to confirm that,' he said. 'We haven't been able to trace any relatives, except his mother, and she's in an old peoples' home. What I would like you to do is to identify the body.'

'I'd rather not,' I said.

'It is important,' he said, 'or I wouldn't trouble you.'

'What about the Army?' I said. 'Or the prison authorities. There must be hundreds of people who knew him better than I did.'

'But you are the most recent contact,' he said. 'And he was intimate with your father.'

'I don't know about intimate,' I said.

'The body's at Pringbourne mortuary,' he said. 'Could you meet me there? If it's any help I could arrange with your local police to lay on a car.'

The thought of a police car arriving in the village to pick me up appalled me. In no time every one of the 150 inhabitants of Duck End would be convinced that the foreigner, 'living with that bundle what done the soap on the telly', had been arrested for killing his poor old dad.

'Don't bother,' I said. 'I'll find my own way.'

'Can you make it three o'clock?' he said.

When I told Frances I had to meet Barker at Pringbourne mortuary, she said, 'I'll come with you.'

'There's no need.'

219

'I'll come,' she said. 'I need something to cheer me up.'

★ ★ ★

The mortuary attendant, a foxy little man in a grubby white coat, lifted the plastic sheet that covered the body. I forced myself to look at the head he exposed. There was a yellowish crepe bandage wound round the temple, to hide the bullet wound, I supposed, and another bandage going under the chin to stop the jaw from sagging. The bandages made a frame for the dead, waxy face. I felt sick and I began to tremble. There was a frozen, inert silence, as though the lifting of the sheet had released a paralysing nerve gas.

'Can you identify the deceased?' Barker's muted voice spoke in my ear.

I tried to answer, but I couldn't form the words. I could only produce a strangled grunt.

'Shall I remove the bandages, sir?' asked the attendant helpfully.

'No,' I managed to say. 'No. I recognise him.'

'I must ask you to tell me the name,' said Barker.

'Dorkes,' I said. 'Edwin Dorkes.'

'You're quite certain?'

'Quite certain,' I said.

'Thank you, Mr Rowlands,' said Barker. 'I'm sorry, but it had to be done.'

He put his hand on my shoulder and guided me away. As we left I heard a metallic clang, and glancing back saw the attendant stacking Dorkes into his refrigerated drawer.

We went up a flight of stone steps to a cluttered office with dirty windows where a Dickensian clerk hunched over a desk. There was a coal fire burning in an oldfashioned, black-leaded grate, and after the dank chill of the tiled morgue, it seemed overpoweringly hot and stuffy.

'Never a pleasant business,' said Barker. 'Take a seat, Mr Rowlands. There are one or two forms Mr Higgins would like you to complete. For the Coroner's office . . . just a formality.'

The forms were the colour of the bandages round Dorkes' head. I had difficulty controlling the pen as I wrote answers to a string of civil service type questions, and then signed a declaration of identification. The clerk checked them through and said they seemed to be in order. Barker came with me to the front door.

'Is that all?' I said.

'For the moment,' said Barker. 'You might have to give evidence at the inquest. Depends on the Coroner. We'll be in touch.'

'Do you know who killed him?' I said.

'These inquiries take time,' said Barker.

'I thought at one time,' I said, 'that Dorkes was the bomber . . .'

'Did you?' he said.

'It mystifies me what he was doing with a false passport,' I said.

'We rather think he was on his way to Italy,' said Barker.

'Italy? What makes you think that?'

'Travicom gave us the lead,' he said. 'The airlines' computer. A seat on a flight to Rome was booked for Thursday in the name of Murphy and never used.'

'It's all very peculiar,' I said.

'Mrs Fairchild well, I hope?' said Barker.

'Quite well, thank you.'

'Ah . . . yes . . . well,' said Barker. He held out his hand. 'Thank you for your help, Mr Rowlands.'

It was a relief to get out into the cold, fresh air. I walked briskly back towards the centre of the town where I had left the Morgan and Frances. She said she was going to look round the shops, and we had arranged to meet at a teashop in the Market Square called Pam's Pantry.

I stopped at the Post Office and went into one of the telephone kiosks. The number of the old peoples' home at Brentwood was in my father's address book. I dialled the number and was answered by a refined contralto.

'Holly Lodge.'

'Is that the . . . er . . . the matron?' I asked.

'Yes. This is Mrs Manners. Can I help you?'

'My name's Charles Rowlands,' I said. 'My father was Colonel Rowlands.'

'Colonel Rowlands?' the contralto rose a tone. 'You're his son? I can't tell you how shocked I was . . . '

'Yes,' I cut in, 'it was a great shock. What I'm actually calling about is Mrs Dorkes.'

'Ah, yes. Dear Mrs Dorkes. The Colonel was so good to her.'

'I'm afraid I have some more sad news,' I said. 'Have the police been in touch with you?'

'The police? No . . .'

'They probably will be,' I said. 'Mrs Dorkes' son, Edwin, has been killed.'

'Good gracious! But how dreadful! Of course, I knew she had a son, but I've never seen him. An army man, I believe. Was he killed in action?'

'Something of the sort,' I said.

'Oh dear, oh dear,' she sighed. 'Ireland, I suppose . . .'

'You say you've never seen him?'

'No,' she said. 'I can't recall him ever visiting his mother. I always thought it rather sad. Not that she would have known who he was. Her poor old mind's quite gone, I'm sorry to say. Quite harmless, of course, and no trouble at all; but she lives in her own little world.'

'I was worried about the money,' I said.

'I understand my father . . . '

'Oh, that's all taken care of,' she said. 'My husband deals with the business side, but I know Colonel Rowlands made arrangements some time ago for payment to be made through his bank — well, a bank, anyway. I rather think it's Swiss. My husband would know the details.'

'You receive payment through a Swiss bank?'

'Zurich,' she said. 'That's Swiss, isn't it? As I say, Mr Manners deals with that side of things. It really is most sad about Mr Dorkes, but you needn't worry about his mother. She wouldn't understand. A mercy, perhaps.'

'Yes,' I said. 'A great mercy. Thank you Mrs Manners. I expect the police will be in touch with you.'

'I'll tell my husband,' she said. 'So kind of you to call.'

Pam's Pantry was an olde worlde establishment with bay windows, a beamed ceiling and rickety tables, mainly occupied by Pringbourne housewives stuffing gooey cakes into their mouths with attempted elegance. I looked round for Frances, and, at first, because I expected her to be alone, I couldn't see her. Then I spotted her at a corner table, in conversation with a man. His back was to me but I recognised at once, and with intense annoyance, who it was. They were so absorbed, they didn't realise I had arrived until I reached their table.

'Not you again!' I said.

Frances coloured; she looked confused and, I thought, a little guilty. But Reece was as irritatingly nonchalant as ever.

'Hello, there, Charles!' he greeted me. 'Hello! How nice to see you. Do join us. Have a meringue.'

'What the hell are you doing here,' I said, sitting down between them.

'Just happened to be in the district,' he said. 'Met Frances, by a happy chance, outside Woolys.' He waved to a passing waitress. 'You'll have some tea? I wouldn't mind another cup, myself. These cakes are delicious, but terribly thirst-making. How about you, Frances?'

Frances shook her head. She seemed curiously subdued and nervous. Reece ordered a pot for two, and then selected an éclair from the plate on the table and bit into it.

'Can't resist these things,' he said. 'Terribly wicked, I know.'

'Was it Dorkes?' said Frances suddenly.

'It was Dorkes.'

'Poor chap didn't get very far, did he?' said Reece. 'Wherever he was going.'

We were silent while the waitress delivered the tea. Frances poured out and handed me a cup. 'Julian thinks he can find out about Frank,' she blurted out abruptly.

'Frank?' I said.

'You know,' she said. 'Julian thinks he can find out whether he's been shot.'

'We have a pretty good line to Rhodesia,' said Reece. 'If he was shot by the Terrs, it shouldn't be too difficult.'

'She only dreamed he was shot,' I said.

'I want to know where I stand!' declared Frances aggressively.

'She doesn't even know if he went to Rhodesia,' I said.

'Of course I do,' said Frances, and gave me a painful kick on my ankle.

'I've just had a splendid idea!' Reece

flashed his show-biz teeth. 'Why don't we make a night of it. Go somewhere for a few drinks and a super meal?' He turned his searchlight on to me. 'We could swap yarns about dear old Uplands, and Frances could tell me more about Frank.'

'Sounds grotesque,' I said dourly.

'Sounds great,' said Frances. 'I haven't had a super meal for God knows how long.'

'There's a place not far from here on the A.11,' enthused Reece. 'The Old Priory. It was featured in the Sunday Times colour supplement.'

'Never read it,' I said. 'Will HMG be paying?'

'Certainly not,' said Reece, with mock severity. 'Most irregular.' Then his disarming smile lit up again. 'I'll pay. This is an invitation. Let's call it a celebration party.'

'What have we got to celebrate?' I asked.

'Ah!' said Reece. 'There must be something. Can you suggest something, Frances?'

'Offhand,' she said, 'I can't.'

'Then it will have to be my promotion,' he said.

'Oh, no!' I said. 'Don't tell me you've been promoted.'

'I'm not absolutely certain,' he said. 'No one actually tells you. You just suddenly find you've got a bigger piece of carpet under your desk. I had the distinct impression this morning that my carpet was bigger than it was yesterday.'

Frances laughed; she seemed to find the idiot amusing.

'That's settled, then,' said Reece. He looked at his watch. 'If we tootle along at a leisurely pace, the bar should be open by the time we get there.'

'I'm going to the loo,' said Frances. 'I've drunk so much tea my bladder's bursting.'

When she had left us in search of relief, I lit a cigarette, while Reece devoured the last remaining fancy cake.

'Charming girl,' he said. 'Frankly, I don't know what she sees in you. Not much justice in the world, is there?'

'That's something to be thankful for,' I said.

'By the way,' he said casually, 'how are you getting on with that jigsaw of yours?'

'I've given up jigsaws,' I said.

'Nasty things,' he said. 'There should be a health warning on every box.'

'If you're going to spend the evening talking about jigsaws,' I said, 'then you can count me out. I don't want to hear any more about bombs or bodies or bloody offshoots thereof. From now on, I'm taking your advice — I'm sticking to the Porker family.'

'Well, the plots are certainly simpler.'

'I know. You already told me.'

Reece finished his cake and dabbed flecks of ersatz cream from his mouth with a blue silk handkerchief.

'Are you and Frances planning to get married?' he said.

'That's something else I don't want to talk about,' I said.

'You are a difficult chap to please,' he said.

13

The Old Priory was mediaeval plastic, with musak piped everywhere, even into the lavatories, which were labelled Monks and Nuns. I wasn't in the mood for this sort of whimsy, and the deep-frozen, micro-waved food did nothing to relieve my sour depression. Frances and Reece, however, seemed to find it all that the colour supplement said it was. After some initial attempts to include me in the conversation, they seemed happy to ignore me, and the evening developed into a private charm contest between the two of them, which I found quite sickening.

I drew some slight consolation in my misery when Reece was presented with the staggering bill, although even this satisfaction was diminished when he flourished an American Express card with an insouciance which Frances obviously admired, reminiscent of television commercials.

The disastrous meal did at least have the effect of hardening my resolve to get on with my own life and my own work, and to resist any further distractions.

My nerves were still on edge, and I jumped, heart in mouth, every time the phone rang; but apart from two wrong numbers and a call from Frances' agent, Max Blumenthal, to say he might fix her up in a new oven cleaner series, there was nearly a week of undisturbed peace. I immersed myself in the adventures of the Porker Family, and settled back into my old comfortable, undramatic routine.

And then, late on Sunday evening, when I was snoozing in front of the fire through a John Wayne 'Western', the telephone erupted, waking me up with a panic-stricken jerk which sent Clive catapulting off my lap.

'Probably Max,' said Frances. 'He said he'd ring.'

She went out into the hall to answer the call, and her first words seemed to confirm my worst fears.

'Why, hullo, Julian,' she said.

I couldn't hear any more of the

conversation because she kicked the door shut, but I knew in my bones that my brief period of peace was over.

'What's happened?' I asked fearfully when she came back. 'What's happened now?'

'Nothing's happened,' she said calmly. 'That was Julian. He thinks he may have traced Frank to the Selous Scouts.'

'Selous Scouts?'

'In Rhodesia,' she said.

'Good God!' I was furious. 'You mean the bastard phoned in the middle of the night, frightening me to death, just to tell you that?'

'It's only eleven,' she said. 'Very decent of him to take the trouble.'

'Was that all?'

'Oh, he invited us to lunch on Tuesday. Bertelli's in Old Compton Street.'

'Bloody nerve!' I said. 'I hope you told him where he got off.'

'No need to come if you don't want to,' she said. 'I've got to see Max, anyway, so I can combine the two.'

'I'm certainly not going to let you two play footsie in Soho,' I said. 'Not after the exhibition you made of yourselves at the Old Priory.'

'Well, it's something to know you're jealous,' she said. 'I was beginning to think you didn't care.'

'Don't flatter yourself!' I said. 'If that's the sort of thing you fancy, you're welcome to it.'

'Are we going to quarrel?' she said, as though, if we were, she needed time to make adequate preparations.

I subsided. I slumped back in my chair.

'Get the whisky, girl,' I said. 'And for Christ's sake shut up.'

'Let's have it in bed,' she suggested.

'So long as the blanket's on,' I said.

*   *   *

By the time Tuesday came round, I had decided I might as well go with Frances. I told myself that it would be a good opportunity to call in at the flat, check that everything was in order and collect any mail that had accumulated.

We got to London at ten in the morning, and I dropped Frances off in

Cambridge Circus where Max had his office, arranging to meet her in Soho at one o'clock.

I drove to Vernon Mews and was relieved to find that the flat, as far as could be seen, was just as I had left it. There were three letters on the mat, and when I had switched on the electric fire, I sat down and opened them. Two were circulars, from the Great Classics Book Club and a double glazing contractor. The third letter was from the treasurer of the Imperial Services Club, a Major G. H. Purdy (Ret'd.). It had been brought to the Major's attention that my father's annual subscription was two months overdue, a sad state of affairs which he was confident my father would wish immediately to remedy.

This letter seemed typical of the old dodderers I had observed at the club, and I wondered how long a member had to be dead before they stopped dunning him for his subscription. It brought back vividly to my mind the day my father had introduced me to the porter, and the self-important geriatrics who had interrupted with their querulous demands. 'Any messages for me, George?' 'Get me a cab, George, there's a good chap.' 'George! Where's me umbrella?'

I remembered, too, how forcibly it had struck me that my father hadn't called the porter George; he'd called him Mr Pond, and the porter, gazing at my father with hero-worshipping eyes, had called him Colonel.

It came to me then, the connection that I knew existed, but hadn't been able to place, between my father and goats.

I jumped up and began to pace about the room, my heart racing with the shock and excitement of the revelation. Of course! Pond had retired and gone to live in Italy with his Italian wife who couldn't speak a word of English. I recalled my father admitting, as we ate braised sheeps' hearts in the club dining room, that he had helped Pond to buy a little farm on the outskirts of Rome.

'A smallholding, really,' he'd said. 'Nothing much, goats and that sort of thing.'

When I'd questioned the wisdom of his philanthropy, his eyes had pleaded with me, begging me to understand.

'An investment, in a way,' he'd said. 'Somewhere to go if things get tiresome . . . '

Was this what Dorkes had been trying to tell me — that my father was alive and holed up in a safe house he had prepared for himself if things got tiresome?

If my father were alive, then who had been blown up and incinerated in the old Rover? The obvious deduction was that it had been Radowski's missing lodger, the Kjanek traitor. But in that case, who had set up the elaborate deception. Who had planted the false clues — the ring, the watch, the shoe — designed to lead to the presumption that my father had been killed? Only my father himself, or Dorkes, could possibly have done this, with, perhaps, the help of Lenisec. But why? If the object had been to eliminate the traitor, it seemed an extraordinary clumsy way of going about it.

One thing, at least, was clear to me now. I could no longer stand aside and tell myself I wasn't involved. I had always been involved, in the nightmares, in the bungled attempts at suicide, in the aura of legendary heroism which surrounded him like a barrier that kept him beyond my reach. If he were alive, I had to find him. I had to know the truth, because it was also the truth about myself.

I wasn't thinking logically. From any rational standpoint, the plan that formed in my brain was crazy. But I was no longer in control; a force outside myself impelled me to leap into the unknown, as my father had leapt, before I was born, into the night sky over Yugoslavia. I was making my own blind drop.

I phoned Bertelli's and left a message for Frances saying that I had been called away urgently. Then I closed the flat and drove to Sloane Street. At a travel agent I booked myself on a flight to Rome from Heathrow at 1700 hours. I was left with five hours to dash back to Duck End, pack a bag, collect my passport and then dash back to London to catch the plane.

I did it with a few minutes to spare, exhausted, hungry and already regretting the impulse that had driven me to embark on such a rash and ill-considered adventure. The small voice, warning me to leave things alone, not to interfere, grew progressively louder, and by the time we touched down at Fiumicino it was shrieking in my brain. I ought to have heeded it; I ought to have taken the first flight home. But now I had jumped, I had to go through with it; there was no going back.

I went to one of the public telephones in the airport arrival hall and dialled the number listed in my father's book under Pond. It was a long time before anyone answered, and then a woman's voice, faint and quavering, said '*Pronto?*'

'I want to speak to Colonel Rowlands,' I said, speaking Italian, for I guessed this was Pond's wife.

There was a lengthy silence. 'I don't understand,' she said at last. 'You have a wrong number.'

'Tell him Mr Murphy wants him,' I said.

Again there was silence. I fed some more coins into the machine and waited. I waited so long, I decided she must have cut me off, and I was about to abandon the call, when I heard the voice I had thought I would never hear again.

'Edwin!' my father said. 'Edwin!'

It was dreadful and uncanny hearing that voice from the dead. I was too choked with emotion to respond.

'Edwin?' he said anxiously. 'Is that you, Edwin?'

'It's not Edwin, father,' I managed to say. 'It's Charles — your son Charles.'

'Charles!' the shock and disappointment were painfully evident. 'What in God's name . . . '

'Edwin's dead, father,' I said.

'Dead?'

'I must see you,' I said. 'I must see you, father.'

'Don't come here!' His voice was sharp with fear. 'Where are you?'

'At the airport.'

'Have you been followed?'

'No. I've just landed. No one knew I was coming.'

'Don't come here!' he said again, and then, hopeless and bewildered, 'Edwin dead?'

'I want to see you,' I said. 'I want to

help you. Can we meet somewhere?'

'Tomorrow,' he said. 'Tomorrow morning. The Stazioni Termini . . . in the subway. Be sure you're not followed.' And then the phone went dead.

I took a taxi into the centre of Rome and spent a sleepless night in a little hotel near the Piazza Argentina. Early next morning, while it was still dark, I joined a chattering throng of office cleaners and workmen on a bus going to the Stazioni Termini. At a halfway point I eased my way towards the central exit and waited until the last disembarking passenger had gone. Then, just before the driver pulled the door closing lever, I leapt out after them. No one followed me. I waited in the cold drizzle for the next bus and it was just after seven when I reached the station. The morning rush from the suburbs hadn't got under way, and the vast concourse of Mussolini's self-aggrandising monument echoed with emptiness. I went down the concrete steps into the subway which led nowhere except to lavatories, a barber's shop and a café that never seemed to open.

241

He was standing in the shadows against the wall, his coat collar turned up, the brim of his soft hat pulled down. As I moved towards him he looked up, and the yellow glare of the electric light fell on his face, sculpting the deep lines of age and tiredness. He saw me, and for a split second the harshness of his expression softened with recognition. And then he was looking beyond me, transfixed with terror.

'No!' he shouted. 'No! Get away, boy! Get away!'

The shots came from behind me, sending shock waves reverberating along the tunnel. He was flung back against the wall; stayed suspended there for a moment, and then crumpled, sliding down and sprawling on the ground.

I wheeled round and glimpsed a squat figure in a blue raincoat disappearing up the steps. I didn't see his face but I knew it was Lenisec.

I went to my father and knelt beside him. The bullets had hit him in the chest. Bloodstains were appearing, developing gradually like a photograph, dark on the grey cloth of his coat, bright red on his shirt. I tried to lift him up, my arm under his shoulders. His innocent violet eyes searched my face, surprised, pained and glazing over.

'Where have you been, Edwin?' he croaked.

'It's Charles, father.' I said. 'It's Charles . . . '

For a moment his eyes cleared. They became bright and feverish. His hands clutched me convulsively.

'Charles . . . ' he gasped. 'I'm finished boy. I'm finished.'

'Why, father?' I said. 'For God's sake, why?'

He was growing weaker; his lips moved and I bent down, trying to catch the faint sounds.

'I went for the water,' he whispered. 'God forgive me, boy — I went for the water.'

He sagged against my arm; his head rolled limply and his eyes lost their colour and went blank. I knew he was dead.

I lowered him gently to the ground, and for the first time I became aware that a small crowd had gathered round, garrulous, gesticulating, but keeping their distance. Suddenly they went quiet and started to move away. I heard a warning murmur '*Polizia!*', and, straightening up, I glimpsed the uniform, the jackboots and the brandished revolvers of approaching *carabinieri*. As the spectators faded away along the tunnel, I faded with them. There was no point in staying; there was nothing I could do for him now.

A train had just come in, disgorging its load of commuters. I merged with the crowd hurrying towards the exit. I felt cold and shivery, but at the same time I was clammy with sweat. I was in a state of numbed shock, and my dominant emotion was one of resentful anger. The words 'I went for the water' throbbed insistently in my brain, telling me I had been cheated. All my life, I felt, I had been defrauded; being judged, and judging myself, against the hero of Kjanek, and always being found wanting. And it had all been a lie.

A man in overalls who had followed me from the subway sidled up and tugged at my sleeve. 'Who was he?' he said. 'Did you know him?'

'No,' I said, roughly shaking free from his clutch. 'No. He was a stranger.'

The man recoiled, wary and suspicious. I had answered in English, but it was the truth in any language.

The jumbled pieces of the jigsaw began to click together in my mind. There were gaps that I filled by guesswork, and others that probably would never be filled; but the main outline of the picture was clear. It wasn't an attractive picture, and I didn't want it to be any clearer. I didn't want to see it at all.

My father had gone for the water. He had saved his own skin by leading the Germans to the caves. The other soldier, the young Yugoslav, had escaped, or perhaps been taken prisoner, and no other witnesses had been left alive. The Partisans had accepted my father's story, blaming the other man and featuring himself as the heroic defender, and this wretched deception, once embarked upon, had to be maintained, even to the extent after the war of joining Lenisec's revenge squad. Working with Lenisec my father had in effect been hunting for himself. He must have imagined he would be safer on the inside, and, in any event, the chances that the one man who knew the truth having survived were remote.

But he had survived, and had turned up thirty-five years later, working in a London hospital and lodging in a Brixton doss-house. In the picture I constructed blackmail had been Mr Archie's game, with a letter, exposing my father to the Yugoslavs, held over him as a permanent threat. God knew how long and how much my father had paid; but it was money thrown away once Leniscc got wind of Mr Archie's existence, and began to move inexorably closer to the truth. My father must have known that it was only a matter of time before his elaborate façade of lies and deceit was torn apart and his guilty secret revealed.

In his desperation he had no one to turn to, no one he could trust, except Dorkes, loyal, devoted Dorkes, the professional killer, so clever with his hands. To

Dorkes the solution would have seemed straightforward — liquidate the blackmailer before Lenisec reached him; and at the same time convince him that the hero of Kjanek had been murdered.

The operation wouldn't have daunted an ex-SAS man with Dorkes' experience and expertise, and who would care if a lonely, friendless foreigner like Mr Archie disappeared? Mr Archies disappeared every day and no one bothered.

What my father and Dorkes intended to do afterwards, I could only surmise, but with money stashed away in a Swiss bank, there were plenty of places in the world where they could have joined successful bank robbers and Nazi war criminals in comparatively secure exile. It had been a mad scheme; but then my father had never been exactly sane.

They might have got away with it if it hadn't been for the incriminating letter, and the fact that Lenisec and his telephone engineers were conducting their own investigation into what they believed was my father's killing. They were watching Dorkes, tailed him to

Radowski's, and when he got back to Fulham, ready to take off to join my father in Italy, they were waiting for him. Knowing Dorkes, he wouldn't have surrendered the letter without a fight, and I guessed he had been shot in the struggle, and his body later dumped in Epping Forest.

Outside on the station forecourt, an armoured van was parked. Two policemen lounged beside it, holding their automatic rifles in a bored way, eyeing the throng as though contemplating taking a pot shot at someone just to relieve the tedium. The touts, pedlars and gipsies were starting their day's work, selling American cigarettes, scarves, pictures of the Virgin, and even, despite the icy drizzle, sunglasses. I shouldered my way past them, dodged the congestion of battered green buses and yellow Fiat taxis and made a suicidal dash across the traffic swirling round the Piazza Cinquecento. I reached the safety of the bare, sodden gardens where the proprietors of kiosks and cafés were taking down their shutters, derelict old men and women huddled on the benches, and disreputable cats scavenged amongst the accumulated rubbish.

In the Piazza della Republica a car drew up beside the kerb, ignoring the blasting horns, the imprecations and frantic arm waving of other motorists maddened by the obstruction.

'Get in Rowlands!' a familiar voice shouted. '*Presto*!'

It was Reece. For a moment I stood rooted to the pavement, only vaguely aware of the Roman workers jostling me, the impatient honking and the operatic protests. Beside Reece in the passenger seat was Barker.

'*Presto*!' Reece yelled. '*Presto*!'

I could hear the wail of a police siren in the distance, getting rapidly louder. I moved towards the car, and as I did so I realised there was someone in the back holding the door open for me.

'*Presto* means quick,' said Frances.

I got in beside her and immediately Reece jerked the car away from the kerb and threw it into the traffic tearing down the Via Nationale.

'I know what *presto* means,' I said. 'It's

about the only thing I do know.'

No one answered. Reece was concentrating on his driving; Barker stared fixedly ahead, whilst Frances had her head turned away looking out of the side window. The silence lasted a long time. I glimpsed the monstrous Emmanuele monument, the columns of the Colosseum, and then we were caught up in the early morning maelstrom of traffic along the Lungotevere beside the Tiber. I felt Frances' hand on my arm.

'Someone had to look after you,' she said.

'Mrs Fairchild has been a great help,' said Barker.

'Where are we going?' I said.

'The airport,' said Reece. 'The sooner we get out of here the better.'

'You knew from the start it wasn't my father in that car,' I said accusingly.

'Oh, yes,' said Barker. 'We knew that.'

'Couldn't have been, could it?' said Reece. 'He'd flown to Italy the day before.'

'Why in God's name didn't you tell me?' I said.

'Ah, yes,' said Barker. 'I suppose we owe you an apology. The fact is, at that stage, we didn't know how far you were involved.'

'I wasn't involved at all!'

'But you led us to him in the end,' said Reece.

'You were a bit late,' I said.

'I suppose you've got that jigsaw worked out now,' said Reece. 'You know who it was in the car?'

'You tell me,' I said.

'The Kjanek traitor,' said Reece. 'Radowski's missing lodger. The man who went for the water — remember?'

It was on the tip of my tongue to blurt out: 'You've got it all wrong! He wasn't the traitor!', but I pulled myself up short. If they didn't know, why should I be the one to tell them? Let them solve their own jigsaws. After all, it was what they were paid for.

My self-pitying anger and resentment had dissipated, overwhelmed by a wave of guilt. 'You led us to him in the end,' Reece had said. I had led Lenisec to him, too. By my interfering I had betrayed him as surely as he had betrayed the Yugoslavs in the caves at Kjanek. Lenisec might have pulled the trigger, but it was I who had killed him. The remorse I experienced was made all the more bitter now that I knew the truth. I felt closer to the dead traitor than I had ever done to the live hero. The barrier that had always separated us had gone and I understood him, and sympathised with him, because we were two of a kind. I knew that if I had been in his predicament, the Germans would have broken me as they had broken him, and that if I had been alone, a stranger at the mercy of men to whom pitiless revenge was a way of life, I would have told the same lies.

'We can't leave him!' I cried out in a sudden panic. 'We can't leave him under Mussolini's bloody station!'

'Who?' said Barker.

'My father. Colonel Rowlands.'

'Unknown man,' said Reece. 'Forged papers.'

'The Eyeties will put it down to the Red Brigade,' said Barker.

'They always do,' said Reece.

'When the inquest resumes,' said

Barker, 'we'll produce evidence of identi-fication. No need to confuse the issue.'

'What do you mean?' I was astounded. 'Do you mean evidence that it was my father in the car?'

'Bloody maniacs!' snarled Reece, swerv-ing violently to avoid a Mercedes that had cut in front of us. No one spoke again until we were on the autostrada leading to Fiumicino. Then Reece said, 'Too late in the day to start re-writing history. Don't you agree, Charles?'

I thought about this. I wasn't sure whether the jigsaw was falling apart again, or whether the pieces really belonged to several different puzzles. But it was clear that Reece knew more than he pretended, and that what I was being involved in now was a cover up.

'It's simpler that way,' said Barker.

It occurred to me that Frances had been strangely quiet. I turned to her. 'What do you think?' I asked.

She didn't look at me. 'I think, thank God something's simple,' she said.

At Heathrow there was a Ford Granada from the Foreign Office to meet Reece and a Jag from the Yard for Barker.

'No wonder taxes are ruining the bloody country,' I said, as I stood with Frances and watched them drive away.

She held out her hand. 'Goodbye, then, Charles,' she said formally. 'I'll let you know where to send my things.'

'What do you mean 'goodbye'?' I said. 'We're going back to Duck End.'

'I can't come back with you,' she said.

'Can't? What are you talking about?'

'Julian wouldn't like it,' she said.

'What the hell has it got to do with Julian?'

'We're getting married,' she said. 'As soon as I can get a divorce or he finds out that I'm a widow.'

'You're crazy!' I cried. 'It's ridiculous! Why marry that creep?'

'Because he asked me,' she said. 'It's as simple as that.'

So something else was simple. Things seemed suddenly to be getting so simple, it was quite complicated.

THREE DAYS TO LIVE

Robert Charles

Mike Harrigan was scar-faced, a drifter, and something of a woman-hater. With his partner Dan Barton he searched the upper reaches of the Rio Negro in the treacherous rain forests of Brazil, lured by a fortune in uncut emeralds. Behind them rode three killers who believed that they had already found the precious stones. And then fate handed Harrigan not emeralds, but the lives of women, three of them nuns, and trapped them all in a vast series of underground caverns.

THE MURDER MAKERS

John Newton Chance

Julian Hammer wrote thrillers. When people asked him how he thought of all the murders, he would reply that he did them personally first. Thus, when Jonathan Blake called on Hammer to look into the case of a missing person, it did appear that the author might have killed him. Hammer, twisting by habit, twisted the issue so well Blake began to suspect that it was Hammer who was in line to be murdered. But Hammer thought it was likely to be Blake. Both were dead right.

SEA VENGEANCE

Robert Charles

Chief Officer John Steele was disillusioned with his ship; the *Shantung* was the slowest old tramp on the China Seas, and her Captain was another fading relic. The *Shantung* sailed from Saigon, the port of war-torn Vietnam, and was promptly hijacked by the Viet Cong. John Steele, helped by the lovely but unpredictable Evelyn Ryan, gave them a much tougher fight than they had expected, but it was Captain Butcher who exacted a final, terrible vengeance.